Beware, Meg . . .

I bent over my social studies homework.

Without warning, my hand picked up the pen and began to write on the pad in front of me.

I couldn't have resisted even if I had tried, and I was too shocked to try.

My hand didn't write in my handwriting, either. It wrote in a thin, spiky cursive that was like an angry spiderweb.

Beware, Meg, it wrote.

"What?" I whispered.

Beware. Your *time* is up.

"Who are you?" I whispered again.

One who warns.

I was trembling, but my hand was steady. With icy calm it wrote *You are in danger.* Your destruction is at hand.

Books by Ann Hodgman

My Babysitter Is a Vampire
My Babysitter Has Fangs
My Babysitter Bites Again
My Babysitter Flies By Night
My Babysiter Goes Bats
My Babysitter Is a Movie Monster

Stinky Stanley
Stinky Stanley Slinks Again
Stinky Stanley, Superhero

MY BABYSITTER FLIES BY NIGHT

Ann Hodgman

Illustrated by

John Pierard

iBooks for Young Readers

Habent Sua Fata Libelli

iBooks
Manhanset House
Dering Harbor, New York 11965

bricktower@aol.com • www.ibooksinc.com

Library of Congress Cataloging-in-Publication Data
Hodgman, Ann. My babysitter flies by night.
(My babysitter) "A Byron Preiss book."
p. cm.
[1. Young Adult Fiction—Horror. 2. Young Adult Fiction—Vampires 3. Young Adult Fiction—Thrillers & Suspense I. Hodgman, Ann, iII. II. Title. III. Series: Hodgman, Ann. My babysitter.

ISBN 978-1-59687-796-2
2025

MY BABYSITTER FLIES BY NIGHT

Table of Contents

Prologue

I didn't know it then, of course, but he was packing his suitcase. Not that he had much to bring. A change of clothes, all black. A handful of dirt from his native land. A bone-handled knife.

He wouldn't have packed a mirror even if he had owned one. He didn't have much interest in mirrors.

I didn't know it then, but he was wondering what we would think of him. Would we notice how . . . different he was? Would he manage to fit in? To convince the rest of us that he was one of us? He knew that it would be uncomfortable to stand out too much.

I didn't know it then, but he was wondering whether to abandon his plan. Could he really pull this off? Was it wise to travel to such an unfamiliar spot? He had always hated being the center of attention. Now he would have no place to hide.

Back then, I didn't know any of this. But how could I have? And how could I have imagined what would happen when he *did* arrive?

Chapter One

Is there anything worse than a best friend who outgrows you?

Well, sure. Lots of things, I suppose. You could get hit by a car, or your house could burn down, or—well, anyway, *lots* of things could be worse. But at the time it was hard for me to remember any of them.

It was a Tuesday afternoon. The Tuesday after Labor Day, in fact. In my town, Litchfield, Delaware, the Tuesday after Labor Day is the day before the new school year starts. At my school, Pelham Middle School, the Tuesday after Labor Day is known as Black Tuesday.

And for me, Meg Swain, the Tuesday after Labor Day is the day I go to see my best friend, Brooke Donohue, so we can be nervous about the next day together.

But when I saw Brooke, I suddenly got more nervous about the way she looked than about the fact that we were starting school the next day.

"Wow, Brooke! Welcome home! I can't believe it's you," I squealed when my friend answered the door. "Yon look so *different!*"

Brooke leaned against the doorjamb, smiled fleetingly, and smoothed back her curly red hair. "You think so?"

"Totally! You're so ... *sophisticated!*"

Brooke gave a little shrug—a gesture I'd never seen her use before. "Well, Meg, I guess that's what happens when you spend a semester living in France. But goodness, I'm forgetting my manners! Won't you come inside?"

She held open the front door and let me in.

These were more things I'd never seen: Brooke saying things like "goodness" and "Won't you come in?" Or Brooke holding the door open. My friend was talking—and acting—like someone else.

As I followed her into the living room, I had the feeling that she had grown five years older during the six months she'd been away. Which would mean, of course, that she was now five years older than *I* was.

When she gracefully sat down and turned to face me, I felt even younger and cloddier. Could this really be Brooke? The same Brooke who had introduced herself by throwing sand in my eyes when we were both three? The Brooke who'd slept with a raggedy old teddy bear called Shoey until last year? The Brooke who had a fit every time her mother suggested that she wear a dress instead of sweat-pants and a T-shirt?

Sitting across from me now was a completely *new* Brooke. Taller and slimmer than I remembered, she was wearing a tight black leather skirt, a white silk blouse, and black suede shoes. Her unruly hair was tamed with a black satin ribbon, and she was wearing black stockings. *Stockings!*

I'd never seen Brooke wear anything on her feet except holey socks she'd borrowed from her brother. Even her ruddy complexion seemed pure and pale now, as though living in France had bleached it somehow. Or did it just look pale in contrast to the red lipstick she was wearing—

Brooke, who had always made gagging noises whenever anyone in our grade wore makeup?

All at once I realized that while I'd been studying my friend, she had been studying me, too. But I couldn't tell what she thought.

"Well," she said after a second, "you haven't changed. Still the same old Meg."

Why did I get the feeling she disapproved of that? What was wrong with being the same old Meg? I was the Meg who had been Brooke's best friend before she'd left for France, after all!

I straightened up in my chair, uncomfortably aware that there was a stain on the neck of my sweatshirt and that my leggings were covered with cat hair. "So how *was* France?" I asked. "Why didn't you ever write? How was your French family? Were there any kids your age? How was the food? How was–"

"Wait, wait!" Brooke interrupted with a silvery little laugh. "That's too many questions at once. Let me start with how France was. I stayed in a suburb of Paris, and ..."

I'm sorry to say that while she was telling me about her trip, my mind drifted. There was a lot *on* my mind, I guess. I had just come back from summer vacation myself, and I was still exhausted from battling vampires....

Yes, that's what I said. And while I'm sure you'd love to hear what Brooke told me about her trip to France, you're going to have to pay attention to me instead. Otherwise the stuff I tell you later won't make any sense.

My family–Dad, Mom, me, my younger brother, Trevor, and our tubby cat, Pooch–always spend the summer on a tiny island off the coast of Maine called Moose Island. Until a year ago, Trevor and I did all the normal island things: swimming, biking, playing in the woods, hunting for arrowheads, picking blueberries, stubbing our toes, scratching bug bites—you get the idea.

Then, last summer, we added a new activity: fighting off vampires. No, I know that's not what most kids do on vacation. But when a vampire wanders into your life, it doesn't leave you a lot of time for berry picking.

Our vampire was a tall, corpselike teenager named Vincent Graver. Vincent started out as our babysitter, if you can believe it. (That was a whole year ago, before my parents let me babysit Trevor myself.)

We managed to vanquish Vincent. Then, this past summer, he managed to come back. *We* vanquished him again, and a few weeks later *he* managed to come back once more. The third time we vanquished him was just two weeks before the first day of school. We hoped that this time it would stick.

I'm leaving out the exciting parts of the summers, but trust me, there was more than enough excitement for everyone. And more than enough neck biting, and blood, and bats.

In fact, there had been so much vampire stuff in the past two summers that I was almost feeling happy about going back to school. School would have to be more relaxing than vacation had been. School would seem nice and reassuring: new notebooks, gleaming blackboards, a pristine empty locker.

At the end of the day I'd have my nice comfortable house: apples ripening on the tree in the front yard, Pooch snoring and whuffling under the sofa, Mom's cheery note on the kitchen counter telling me and Trevor not to touch any of the brownies in the fridge. (We would conveniently lose the note until after we had finished the brownies, of course.) Even homework would seem like a pleasant change from stuffing vampires into coffins.

An island is different. Probably you should expect adventures on an island. But Litchfield, Delaware, isn't an adventure place. It's just regular. It's *home.* Nothing exciting happens here—and certainly nothing scary.

Brooke's thoughts seemed to have been running in the same direction. "Litchfield's sure going to seem quiet now," she complained. "I hope that when we get *our* foreign-exchange student, he won't be bored out of his mind."

That took my mind off my vacation. "What foreign-exchange student?" I asked.

Brooke acted startled. "You didn't know that a foreign-exchange student is coming to our school this year? Boy, I really *did* forget to write, didn't I? It was part of the deal with me going to France. He'll spend a semester with us, just like I spent a semester in France."

"It's a boy?" I asked dopily.

"Yes, but that's all I know about him. He's been in the U.S. for a week already, touring around with other foreign-exchange students. Mom's picking him up at the airport tomorrow."

"Picking him up?" I repeated.

"To come to my house." I must still have seemed confused because Brooke added, "He's going to be *living* at my house."

"Since when? I mean, when did you find out about all this?"

"During the summer sometime," Brooke said. "Mom wrote me to let me know the plan. I really didn't tell you anything about it?"

I shook my head.

"Well, goodness." (There she went saying "goodness" again.) "Sorry, Meg. I thought everyone would know about it by now. Of course it won't make much difference. I mean, he'll just be here for the first semester. And I don't even know if I'll like him. He could be a total loser."

Yes, but he probably wouldn't be. I was sure that total losers *never* got exchanged, or went on foreign exchanges, or whatever you call it. This boy would probably be just as suave and sophisticated as Brooke now was.

And if Brooke had gotten all interested in clothes and makeup while she was away, she had probably gotten interested in boys, too. And with a suave foreign student living *right in her house*, she wouldn't have to look far for romance.

I'm not a disloyal friend. Really I'm not. If Brooke wanted to change her image, it was fine with me. (I think.) But did changing her image mean leaving me behind?

It sure seemed like it.

Chapter Two

"Everything will be fine, Meg," my mother said reassuringly. "You should try to eat some breakfast, honey. And if you can't eat, at least drink your orange juice."

"I can't, Mom," I wailed. "It's making my throat close up!"

My younger brother, Trevor, looked up from his Honey Smacks with interest. "Cool! My juice doesn't do that," he said. "Can I try some of Meg's?"

First day of school. I'm sure you know what it's like. Your stomach hurts, your hair looks as though someone tried to fold it, you don't know what to wear, you have to smile like a moron while your parents take your picture on the front steps of your house.

And smeared on top of all these not-so-fun feelings is the even-less-fun feeling that one more golden summer is gone forever and one more grayish-brown school year is about to trap you in its net. The day before, I had almost been looking forward to school. Now I realized I must have been crazy.

As first days of school go, this was a pretty one, sunny and crisp. But I was too far gone to think about the weather.

When the front doorbell rang, it startled me so much that I threw my orange juice all over my father's shirt.

"That must be Brooke," I said nervously. (Brooke always picked me up so we could wait at the bus stop together.) "Oh, no! I'm not ready!"

Dad stared down at his wet shirt and shook his head. "Lucky *I'm* not going anywhere special today," he said mildly, dabbing at his shirt with a napkin. My father is a screenwriter. (My mother is in her final year of medical school.) Sometimes Dad works 'round the clock, and sometimes he just sits and watches the sports channel on cable. I guess this was going to be one of his sports-channel days.

"I'll clean up the floor for you, Meg," Mom offered. "You go get the door."

I had hoped that during the night, Brooke would change back to her old, unsophisticated self. When I opened the door, I saw that this wish had not been granted. Brooke was wearing a sleeveless black leather jacket, very tight, and a short black denim skirt, also very tight. I noticed that she had had a manicure. Her nails were long, curved, and dark red, like talons dipped in blood.

"Gracious, Brooke!" Mom had come up behind me to say hello. "Is that really what you're wearing to school?"

"I guess it is, Mrs. Swain," Brooke said coldly. She turned to me. "Are you ready, Meg?"

"Just give me one sec," I answered. I tore upstairs, brushed my teeth, grabbed my backpack off my desk, tripped, fell down the stairs, and landed in a heap at Brooke's feet.

The old Brooke would either have laughed or been sorry for me. The new Brooke just rolled her eyes and said, "Well, I can see *this* day is off to a great start."

Which was just the way I was feeling, too.

"Hi, Brooke! Wow! Did you have a makeover or something?"

"Brooke, you look fabulous!"

"*Trés chic,* Brooke!"

"*Whit—wheeee-ew!*" (Or however you spell someone whistling.)

That was what greeted me and Brooke when we arrived at homeroom. Or what greeted the new Brooke, I should say. No one seemed to notice I was there.

"Welcome back, Brooke! When will your guest arrive?" asked our homeroom teacher.

"Around ten," Brooke told her, sliding gracefully into the seat next to me. "Mom will meet his plane, take him home to drop off his stuff, then bring him here for the rest of the day."

"Who? Whose stuff? What guest?" asked Miriam Charney, turning around in her seat to stare at Brooke. Miriam's a little obnoxious.

"Brooke's going to be hosting a foreign-exchange student for the first semester," Mrs. Schultz explained. He's a seventh grader, just like you. It will be up to you all to make him feel at home. Remember, no matter what country we come from, we're all the same underneath. Because we're all—"

Miriam threw her hand into the air and waved it frantically. "I can't figure out my schedule," she said when Mrs. Schultz called on her. "They've given me gym at the same time as math. Can you help me? I'll get in *trouble* if I skip math!"

Mrs. Schultz sighed. Maybe she was sad that her little speech had gone unnoticed. But when she started explaining about our new schedules, and how the office computer had messed everything up, and how it would be a few days before everything got sorted out, the talk about our foreign-exchange student kind of drifted away.

Later, when the new student actually arrived, I'm sure Mrs. Schultz wondered whether all of us really *are* the same underneath. On the surface, he was awfully different from the rest of us.

* * *

Mrs. Schultz doesn't *only* have a homeroom, of course. She also teaches Spanish, which both Brooke and I have taken since fourth grade. That's how I was there when Brooke's mother brought the new student to join our class.

"Hi, guys," said Mrs. Donohue, Brooke's mom. "I'd like you to meet Voldar Constantin. Voldar is from the country of Drazylvonia, in the Carpathian Mountains. Voldar, these are some members of your new class."

The boy stepped to the center of the room and bowed low. "Greetings, fellow students," he said in a deep, hollow voice. "I am honored to make your acquaintance."

Amazingly, no one laughed. I think we were all too surprised at the way Voldar looked to notice the way he talked.

Where should I start? He was dressed all in black, but maybe that wasn't so unusual. I mean, maybe fashions were different in his country. Besides, Brooke was wearing all black that day, too.

But Voldar was very, very tall—much taller than the average seventh-grade boy. He was also very, very pale—so pale his skin was almost gray. He had black, glittering eyes, deep-red lips, and—

No. It couldn't be.

He couldn't have pointed teeth.

But he did. When Mrs. Schultz welcomed him to the class, Voldar smiled at her, and I saw that I was right. His teeth *were* pointed. Not like cat's teeth or anything, but definitely not flat on top.

Mrs. Schultz was determined to pretend everything was normal. "Class, why don't you tell Voldar your names and a little bit about yourselves?" she asked. (That horrible teacher trick! Why do they do it to us?) Smiling at Voldar, Mrs. Schultz added, "Now, I don't expect you to remember all these names right off the bat."

"Off the—bat?" Voldar repeated, frowning slightly. He had just a trace of an accent.

"Oh, that's an expression, Voldar." Mrs. Schultz looked flustered, but she recovered quickly. "All right, class. Mike, you may begin."

"Uh, I'm Mike Cleary, and I—uh—play soccer...."

"I'm Dorrie Richards, and I'm vice president of the student council...."

"I'm Rad Montgomery, and I want to make a lot of money...."

Brooke's turn came before mine. "I'm Brooke Donohue, and you're going to be living at my house this semester," she said with just the right touch of cool in her voice.

Voldar bent his head courteously—almost a bow, but not quite. "Really! I am enchanted to meet you, Brooke," he said. "I look forward to getting to know you better."

Miriam Charney let out one of her loud, obnoxious giggles.

Voldar whipped around and aimed a searing glance at her—and everyone in the room froze.

Except in the movies, I had never seen such a frightening change on a person's face. Suddenly Voldar was more gargoyle than person.

"I said something funny?" Voldar hissed, drawing himself up so that he seemed to loom over us.

"N-no! Of course not! I—I didn't mean anything!" Miriam faltered. And she shrank back in her seat like a scared rabbit.

"It is your custom to laugh at gratitude to one's host?" he said.

"No way!" Miriam squeaked.

"In my country we take these hospitalities very seriously." Voldar drew a breath, and suddenly his hard expression disappeared. With a smile he turned to the person behind Brooke.

I saw Mrs. Schultz give a sigh of relief. It wouldn't have started her year off very well if our school's first foreign-exchange student had murdered one of our seventh graders.

I was in the last row, so you'd think I would have had plenty of time to think of "a little bit about myself." When my turn came, though, my mind instantly went blank. Did I *have* any interests? I couldn't remember.

"My name is Meg Swain," I blurted out, "and I, um, I just got back from vacation."

"Well, big whoop," I heard someone whisper. "So did everyone else in the room."

Voldar paid no attention to the whisperer. He was staring intently at me.

Once again I shuddered. What was it about Voldar's face? Was there some kind of . . . power in his eyes?

For a long moment Voldar was silent. Then—"Your name is quite familiar, Meg," he said slowly. "Why?"

I tried to return his gaze, but it was so intense that I had to look away. "I don't know," I said weakly. "Why?"

"No doubt I will remember before long," said Voldar, and then he switched his attention to the boy behind me.

Whew. I felt as though I'd been dropped on the floor and left in a heap like a rag doll. As though I'd narrowly escaped danger.

But had I? Was I, perhaps, still *in* danger?

And was I the only one?

The only empty desk in the room was right behind Brooke, so naturally Voldar sat there. As Spanish went on, I couldn't help darting occasional glances at him. I had the uneasy feeling that I should be keeping track of him.

Not that he was doing anything dangerous. He was just sitting there, staring at Brooke's neck.

Wait a minute, I suddenly thought. Brooke's *neck?*

There's nothing about Brooke's neck to attract attention. She doesn't have a tattoo or a birthmark. She doesn't wear weird necklaces. She just has a neck.

But there was Voldar, ogling the back of Brooke's plain old neck as though it were some kind of... ripe, delicious fruit, or something. As though he hadn't eaten in months.

Now he was bending closer toward Brooke, his mouth open slightly. He licked his lips, and I could see his white teeth gleaming. (I checked them out again. Yes, they were definitely pointed.)

Closer he leaned, and closer. The look in his eyes could almost have burned a hole in Brooke's skin. I was pretty sure I could *see* his teeth growing longer.

Silently Voldar stretched out a hand. . . .

I must have let out a yelp because Mrs. Schultz looked up. "Voldar, what are you doing?" she asked sharply, zeroing in on him.

"I have never seen a spider like this one," Voldar answered, still bent over Brooke's neck. "I collect spiders, you know. This must be an American species."

He reached out and plucked a tiny speck off Brooke's neck.

Brooke flinched. "There's a spider on me?" she said nervously. "I hate spiders! Get it away!"

Voldar was already folding up the spider—if it *was* a spider—in a piece of paper. He tucked the paper into a pocket and smiled pleasantly.

"It is now away," he told her. "I shall add it to my collection."

"Eeeeeew!" Brooke said with a shudder. Then she seemed to remember that girls who had spent a semester in France didn't say "Eeeeeew" anymore. "Well, thanks for getting it off me, Voldar," she drawled. "I certainly don't want webs all over my clothes."

"No. That would be most unattractive," Voldar agreed. He returned to filling out one of the nine million forms Mrs. Schultz had given him.

But when I peeked back at him again a few seconds later, I noticed that he was frowning. Was he disappointed? Had he hoped for a quick snack—a *bloody* snack—to keep him going?

I gave myself a mental slap in the face. *You're being ridiculous,* I scolded myself. *You're seeing vampires everywhere.*

But even if Voldar hadn't been hoping to snack off Brooke's neck, what kind of person has a spider collection?

And what kind of person drinks his lunch? When he sat down at our lunch table, Voldar pulled a flask out of his pocket. Acting as if it were a perfectly normal thing to do, he started sipping from the flask.

"Voldar, you can't drink in school," scolded Miriam Charney in a scandalized voice. "You'll get expelled!"

Voldar gave her a distant smile. "This is not an alcoholic beverage," he said. "This is a mealreplacing formula from my homeland. It comes in handy on my travels."

"Is it one of those drinks that makes you lose weight?" asked Miriam.

"Not exactly," said Voldar. "It would be too complicated to explain the recipe." He tilted his head back and took a deep drink from the flask.

I watched him closely. And it seemed to me that the minute he swigged down that drink, a little color came into his grayish face.

Almost as if he had just drunk a nice dose of fresh blood.

All right, two examples of vampirish behavior probably wouldn't convince everybody. But they convinced *me*. As I've already reminded you, I've had some experience in these matters.

I was absolutely, positively, completely sure that Voldar was a vampire.

"If it's okay with you, I won't pick you up before school tomorrow," said Brooke that day after school.

"Why not?" I pulled my earth science book out of my locker and turned to face her.

"I'm going to walk to school with Voldar. To show him how to get there from my house," she explained.

"But why can't Voldar take the bus like us? It's kind of far to walk," I pointed out. "It's like five miles, isn't it?"

Brooke shrugged. "He says he prefers walking."

"Well, okay. I'll see you at school, then." I stuffed my books into my backpack and started toward the front door, where the school buses were lined up. But Brooke stayed where she was.

"Aren't you coming?" I asked, turning to her.

"Uh, no." Brooke flushed slightly. "As a matter of fact, I'm walking home with Voldar. To show him how to get to my house from school."

The bus route went exactly the same way they'd be walking. Brooke could have showed Voldar how to walk to her house from the bus—they didn't *have* to walk the route. But I didn't bother arguing with her.

I knew what she was trying to tell me.

Chapter Three

"I need to bring in two pounds of uncooked macaroni and a can of copper spray paint to school," Trevor announced the minute we had all sat down to dinner. "Where can I find them?"

Mom sighed. "We've got half a box of spaghetti in the cupboard, if that'll do you any good. Copper spray paint—no, I don't think so. Can you use markers instead?"

"Markers. *Great.*" My brother is just learning how to be sarcastic. He thinks it's really grownup. "That'll look *great* for the harvest wreath we're supposed to be making. Can't you or Dad take me to a hardware store after supper? I need this stuff for tomorrow."

"Oh, I'm sorry, honey," Mom said. "I don't think any hardware stores will be open this late."

"Uh-huh, they will. Gilder's Home Supplies is open twenty-four hours a day. Ms. Hardy said so. It's this big store out in Leawood."

Mom sighed again. "But Leawood's half an hour away! Oh, Trevor. I was hoping this kind of thing wouldn't start up so soon. ... I guess if you don't mind skipping dessert, there'll be time to take you there."

"What's for dessert?" Trevor asked.

"Come to think of it, I forgot to get anything," my father answered. (It was his turn to make supper.) "You'll have to make do with whatever's in the house already."

"Dad!" Trevor protested. "On our first day of school?"

"Yup," Dad said. "Sorry, Trev. And speaking of school"—he turned to me—"how was *your* first day, Meg? You haven't said much about it. Do you have to bring in any macaroni tomorrow?"

I tried to smile. I hadn't really cheered up since that afternoon. "No. Just a lot of homework."

"How were all your friends?" Mom asked. Before I could answer, she added, "Oh! And how was the new foreign-exchange student?"

Just what I didn't want to tell her about *now.* "He seems okay," I said dismissively. "Not too friendly, but—"

Just then my fork clattered to the floor.

"Sorry," I said. I bent over, picked up the fork, and put it back on my plate. "Anyway, his name is Voldar, and—"

My fork clattered to the floor again. Again, I bent over and picked it up.

"You must be tired, honey," Mom said. "Try to get to bed early tonight, okay?"

For the third time my fork—yes, you guessed it—clattered to the floor.

The thing was, this time I hadn't been *holding* my fork. Which meant that I hadn't dropped it. It had just jumped off my plate by itself.

I was the only person who'd noticed, and of course, I figured I'd imagined it. But the minute I picked up my fork again, my *father's* fork fell to the floor. Then Mom's, then Trevor's.

We all looked at each other. "Okay, who's kicking the table leg?" Dad asked.

We all shook our heads. Our forks were now skittering around on the floor like silvery little crabs.

"Maybe some big truck's going by outside," Mom suggested. "The vibrations might be—"

Just then a lightbulb fell from the ceiling fixture and plinked onto the edge of Mom's plate. It broke into a shower of delicate slivers.

"What's going on here?" Dad asked irritably. "The house is falling apart!"

"Is it really?" my brother asked in a small voice.

"Oh, no, Trev," Dad hastened to assure him. "Something's shaking us up a bit, that's all."

This turned out to be sort of an understatement. At that moment the dining room table began to tremble wildly, shaking the plates off the edge so they crashed to the floor. Trevor's cup of milk tipped and spilled. A plate of sliced cucumbers flipped over and landed upside-down. Pale green cucumber disks slithered bumpily through the rivulets of tomato sauce that were now spreading slowly across the table from a bowl of ravioli.

Pooch had been sleeping under the table. With a frightened yowl, he jumped up and bolted out of the room. I wished I could have followed him, but the floor had started shaking, and I could never have gotten across it without falling.

Then a low, rumbling noise began to drift up from the floor. "This must be an earthquake," my mother said frantically as a dinner roll bounced into her lap. "Kids, get under the table!"

"No, wait!" Trevor said. He was gripping his chair with white-knuckled fingers. "Aren't we supposed to put our heads down on our knees? Like on an airplane?"

"We're not *on* an airplane!" Mom said even more frantically. "Please do as I—"

CRASH! The rest of her words were drowned out as the whole light fixture wrenched loose from the ceiling and smashed onto the table.

We lurched to our feet—as everything stopped. Just *stopped.*

The table stopped shaking and stood there politely, as if it couldn't understand how it had gotten so messy. The cucumbers stopped slithering. My father's water glass, which had been teetering on the edge of the table, suddenly decided to hit the floor. There was a gentle tinkling sound, and then the room was silent.

"My word," Mom breathed at last. "*Was* that an earthquake?"

"It certainly felt like one," said my father, staring up at the ceiling with awe. There was a gaping, ugly hole there now, with lots of dustylooking wires poking out. "But I don't think there's ever been an earthquake around here. Not for the past couple of centuries, anyway."

I exhaled shakily. "How'd we get so lucky *now?*" I asked.

Dad shook his head. "I don't know, Meg. I'd better call the neighbors and see if anything's happened to them."

We watched as he carefully picked his way across the dining room floor toward the hall phone.

"I'll try the Ameses first," said Dad. (They live next door to us.) He picked up the receiver, and—

And dropped it immediately.

Coming out of the receiver, so loud that we all heard it clearly, was a hideous cackle.

Dad took a deep breath and picked up the receiver again. "Who's there?" he shouted into it. "Who *are* you?"

No answer. Just the weird, witchy cackling again.

i

My father hung up, and the sound cut off abruptly. He picked up the receiver again—and for the third time the terrible laughter sawed through the air.

Dad slammed down the receiver. In the throbbing silence that followed, we stared horrified at one another.

"Well," Mom finally said, when nothing else happened, "I guess we'd better start cleaning up this mess."

Half an hour later I was up in my bedroom trying to get started on my homework. Downstairs, Dad was taking the phone apart to see if he could figure out what was the matter with it. Mom and Trevor had gone to the hardware store. Everything was quiet now, but the atmosphere in the house was tense and edgy still, and I was having trouble concentrating.

I was trying to remember exactly at what point all that weird stuff had started happening during supper. I had a feeling it had been when Mom had asked me about "the new foreign-exchange student." Hadn't I just begun answering her when my fork went crazy?

Yes. I was pretty sure I had gotten as far as saying, "His name is Voldar."

Was it possible that somehow Voldar had been trying to stop me from saying anything more?

Oh, come on, I scoffed to myself. *Why would Voldar try to shut you up by throwing forks around?*

I had to admit it didn't make much sense. But it didn't make sense that the table had started shaking for no reason, either. And that voice coming out of the telephone—*that* certainly didn't make sense.

Oh, well. Sitting there worrying about it wasn't going to help anything.

I bent over my social studies homework again.

Name the principal rivers of South America was the first review question I read.

I rubbed my eyes tiredly, trying to remember. Well, the Amazon, of course. And the Orinoco, and–

Without warning, my hand picked up the pen and began to write on the pad in front of me.

I didn't pick up the pen and begin to write. My hand did it without my telling it to, if you know what I mean. I couldn't have resisted even if I had tried, and I was too shocked to try.

My hand didn't write in my handwriting, either. It wrote in a thin, spiky cursive that was like an angry spiderweb.

And it certainly didn't write the names of South American rivers.

Beware, Meg, it wrote.

"What?" I whispered.

Beware. Your time is up.

"Who are you?" I whispered again.

One who warns.

I was trembling, but my hand was steady. With icy calm it wrote *You are in danger. Danger is close by. Evil will swallow you.*

The letters were getting bigger now. Bigger, and darker. *Your destruction is at hand.*

My heart was pounding. I wanted to stop writing–I was desperate to stop writing–but my fingers were clenched around the pen with some sinister power that was not my own.

You will–

The hand–*my* hand–suddenly halted.

"I will what?" I asked aloud.

Suddenly my hand traced a jagged line down the paper, as if someone were yanking it away from the message it was writing. Someone else's hand, not mine, hurled the pen to the ground.

And as I stared, horror-struck, at the writing in front of me, it began to fade. Within seconds it was gone. The sheet of paper was blank again.

No trace remained of the message I had just received. But echoing throughout my room was a weird, witchy cackle.

Chapter Four

“Please pass the milk, Trev,” I said at breakfast the next morning. “No! I said *pass* it, not throw it!”

“I didn’t throw it!” Trevor wailed. “It threw itself right out of the cup!”

A wave of milk had jumped across the table at me, drenching the front of my shirt.

Before I could clean up the milk, there was a clanging sound from the oven. Startled, we all peered over from the kitchen table. The oven door was yawning open and slamming shut all by itself.

As we watched, the front burner on our gas stove flared up. Blue flames leaped into the air, and sparks flew around the kitchen like angry fireflies. Mom hopped up to turn off the burner, but it subsided before she got there.

She sank back into her chair. “If this—whatever it is—starts playing with fire,” she said through clenched teeth, “I’m going to give it a spanking.”

No one in my family was in a particularly great mood that morning. When all the alarm clocks in the house go off at four A.M., and the water in the shower keeps switching from hot to icy, and you walk into the kitchen to find that someone—or something—has cooked itself a bunch of fried eggs on the kitchen floor, you have trouble feeling cheerful.

Before any of us could say anything more, a little music box on the windowsill began to plink out its delicate melody. The ballerina on the top of the box spun around gracefully, blew my mother a kiss, and snapped to attention the instant the music turned off.

The kitchen fell blessedly silent.

"Maybe the thing's apologizing," Dad said.

"Well, the apology is *not* accepted," Mom snapped. "Anyway, what exactly do we think is going on here?"

Dad looked a little sheepish. "Some people might say we have a poltergeist in the house," he said.

"A poltergeist?" piped up Trevor. "What's that?"

I had seen the movie *Poltergeist* (and I highly recommend it), so I knew what to tell him. "A poltergeist is a type of ghost," I said. "Sort of a mischievous type. Poltergeists get into houses and play tricks on the people who live there."

Trevor's eyes were wide. "Tricks like throwing milk on you?"

"That kind of stuff, yes."

"But why?" asked Trevor. "Why would a poltergeist be in *our* house?"

"Oh, poltergeists aren't real, honey," my mother said hastily. "They're just like regular ghosts—they don't exist."

Trevor looked unconvinced. "But the milk throwing exists," he pointed out, "because I didn't throw that milk. Really, I didn't. And I didn't set the alarm clocks or fry the eggs or—"

"Of course you didn't, Trev," said my father. "But a poltergeist didn't, either. There's probably some kind of structural problem with the house. Maybe the roof's about to collapse," he added gloomily. "That would be just our luck. . . .

Oh, I'm not serious about that, either," he said when he saw my brother's face. "I just meant that maybe some of the pipes are shaking or some of the flooring's loose or something. Whatever it is, I'm sure it will stop all by itself."

I didn't volunteer my opinion, but I was sure Dad was wrong. This problem wasn't going to go away all by itself.

What's more, I didn't think a poltergeist was responsible. And I *do* believe in poltergeists. (I mean, I never used to believe in vampires, and look what happened!) But this was no poltergeist, I was positive.

This was Voldar. He was trying to scare me because I had guessed his secret. Of course there was no way of proving it, but I knew I was right.

But if Voldar thought that a bunch of fried eggs was going to scare me, he didn't know me very well. It takes more than fried eggs to scare *me.*

What it takes is having a hideous, ghoulish face leering up at me from the bottom of my cereal bowl. Which is what happened as I spooned up my last bite of cereal.

The bottom of the bowl began to writhe and squirm as if it were coming to life—and as if the china bowl were no thicker than the skin of a balloon. Then the face pressed up through the china, trying to burst out at me. Its pointed teeth were bared in a yowling snarl. One gleaming incisor broke through the surface, and then another....

"Yiiiie!" I screamed, jumping to my feet so fast that my chair toppled over behind me.

"What's the matter, Meg?" my mother asked.

"Oh, nothing," I lied as I straightened my chair. "I just noticed the time."

Then I really *did* notice the time. "Hey, I must've missed the bus!" I exclaimed. "It's twenty after! I'm going to be late!"

"Oh, dear," said my mother. "We were all moving slowly after being woken up so early. Well, go hop in the car. I'll drive you."

Fifteen minutes later she was pulling into the school parking lot. "Do you have everything?" she asked.

"Yup. Thanks, Mom," I said gratefully. I scrambled out of the car, waved a quick goodbye, and raced toward the front door of my school.

The building was discouragingly silent as I ran up the walk. Any other latecomers were already safely inside. Homeroom had started. In fact, it was almost over. Through a window I could see one class finishing the Pledge of Allegiance and sitting down. I hated to be marked late on the second day of the year....

Out of the corner of my eye I caught a flash of movement. Startled, I stopped for a minute. The sight my brain had registered was not possible. People did not climb straight up the sides of brick buildings.

But someone had done just that—was still doing it, in fact. At the far end of the building, twenty feet off the ground, I could see a figure dressed in black scrambling up the wall as nimbly as a bat.

Voldar.

Without stopping to think, I ran to the end of the building and stood underneath him. "What are you doing up there?" I shouted furiously. "Get down!"

Voldar did. Immediately. He let go of the wall and landed catlike in front of me.

"Is there a problem, Meg?" he asked calmly.

"Yes! There is! You're not supposed to—"

I broke off. Was there an actual *rule* saying you couldn't climb up the school? I wasn't sure.

"I don't think we're allowed to climb school property," I finished lamely.

Voldar looked at me. "You are in charge of enforcing the rules?" he asked.

"Of course not," I snapped. "But it's okay for me to tell you you're doing something wrong. Being from a foreign country and all, you should be *glad* that I'm trying to help you out."

"I do not get the feeling, Meg, that you are trying to help me out," Voldar replied. "It seems to me that you are trying to get me into trouble. Are you planning to turn me in to the authorities?"

I wasn't sure what to say. I'm hardly the kind of person who runs around trying to get other people in trouble. So what was I doing, exactly?

I didn't know. I just didn't know. All I knew was that I was furious at Voldar.

"You think I don't know what you're up to, but I do," I said. "And believe me, I won't let you get away with—"

Suddenly I stopped. I had just noticed a ring on Voldar's left hand.

It was made of strange dark metal covered with curlicues that looked like ancient writing. A dark red, oval stone was set in its center.

I had seen a ring very much like it before—only a few months earlier, in fact. The ring I had seen belonged to Vincent Graver.

Vincent, as you may remember, was my "first" vampire: the one I kept trying to vanquish. And Vincent's ring (like Vincent) had had some rather nasty powers. The last I'd seen of the ring, a bat had been carrying it away....

"Where did you get that ring?" I asked.

Voldar whipped his hand behind his back. "Why do you want to know?" he asked in return.

"It looks familiar. Did someone give it to you?"

"Perhaps." Voldar's voice was icy. "Are all Americans so interested in other people's business?"

"Perhaps," I repeated. "But really, Voldar, this is important. *Did* someone give you that—"

"ENOUGH!" Voldar suddenly roared. "Enough of your meddling! Get away from me, or I'll—"

"You'll what? Suck my blood in front of the whole school?" I asked tauntingly.

At that, Voldar seemed to become another person entirely. He loomed up even taller. His face darkened, and I could have sworn sparks leaped out of his eyes. He raised his hands, and for the first time I noticed that his nails were as pointed as his teeth. Then he took a threatening step toward me, and—and I don't know what he did next, because I turned and ran like a rabbit.

The only thought I had, besides wanting to get away from the terrifying being Voldar had become, was that now I was *really* late for homeroom.

"You know, Brooke, I don't want to butt in to your business," I said tentatively at lunch.

"Right." Brooke's tone was curt. She opened a makeup mirror and studied her face, pointedly not looking at me. "So don't."

But I went ahead and butted in anyway. "Have you noticed anything unusual about Voldar?"

"Like what?"

"Well, he—he doesn't seem like a regular kid, does he?" I said.

"Meg, as you may remember, he's not from around here. Besides, does *everyone* have to be a regular kid?" Brooke said ominously. "Can't there be a few *interesting* people in the world?"

"Sure, but I think Voldar is—well—too interesting." I took a deep breath. This wasn't going to be easy. "You know, Brooke, I never got a chance to tell you about my summer."

"What does that have to do with Voldar?" Brooke shut her mirror with a snap.

"It's just that I met someone sort of like Voldar this summer. And if Voldar *is* like this person I met—well, then I think you should stay away from him."

"What's it got to do with you, Meg?" Brooke sounded angrier than I had ever heard her. "Are you such a great judge of character all of a sudden?"

"No!" I protested. "I'm trying to warn you!"

"Well, *stop* trying! Because there's nothing to warn me about! I swear, you kids are all the same."

I think the best word for the way I looked at Brooke would be *goggling*. " 'You kids'?" I repeated. "Aren't you one of us?"

Brooke didn't answer that, I noticed. "I can tell you one thing, Meg." She jumped to her feet. "*Voldar* isn't one of you. He's more mature than the rest of you put together. And he understands me. Maybe it's because we've both lived abroad—"

"Lived abroad?" I interrupted. "Brooke, you were only gone for seven months!"

"It doesn't matter. I can still appreciate a person like Voldar better than you can. He's really smart and really good-looking, and he knows way more about life than the kids in this stupid town. And if you can't see that, Meg, then I just pity you."

Head high, Brooke swept away.

Chapter Five

You don't want to hear about the next few days after Brooke stopped talking to me. Every day would sound the same.

First, there were the calls that Brooke never returned. Her mother would say, "I don't think she can come to the phone now, dear, but I'll have her call you back." Brooke never called back.

Second, there were the mornings and afternoons when I looked out of the bus window and saw Brooke and Voldar walking to and from school arm-in-arm. Neither of them ever glanced up as the bus went by.

Third, there were all the little problems at home—my home, I mean. The poltergeist, or the shaky heating system, or whatever it was, acted up all the time.

My family and I woke to drawers opening and closing, popcorn popping itself (inside the kitchen cupboard), windowpanes cracking. We went to bed with window shades flapping, smoke detectors screaming, clock hands whirring around clock faces like something in a cartoon. The house danced and quivered. It knocked on its own walls. It shook pictures off their hooks and sent them smashing to the floor.

And then it began to seem that the house's activities were getting more violent. As if the poltergeist was learning how to do its job better—or trying to scare us harder. Or both.

I mean, when the knives in the knife rack jump out and do a little dance about two inches from your face, that's not quite the same kind of thing as frying eggs on the floor. And when chairs started to break under us, and blasts of heat chased us from room to room, and the car backed itself out of the garage with no one inside, I was sure the poltergeist was upping the ante.

"I can't take this anymore," my mother said one morning. She looked exhausted, which wasn't surprising considering that our piano had been playing the "Twilight Zone" theme song all night long. "We have to do something."

"Like what?" asked Trevor listlessly. He was resting his head on the table.

"Move. Bomb the house. *Anything* to get our lives back to normal."

"You're right. This has to stop. I'll find an engineer to check things out," my father promised.

Dad had to borrow a neighbor's phone to make the appointment. (Our own telephone had stopped cackling by then, but now every number we dialed hooked us up with the Dial H for Horror Hotline.) But when Dad came home and triumphantly announced that he'd found an engineer who would come the next day, we all felt better. Mom said, "We can all manage without sleep for one more night, can't we? Well, *can't we?*"

"C'mon, gang, you can do it! C'mon, gang, you can do it!"

I have often wished that our gym teacher, Mrs. Brockler, knew how to be more inspiring. When you have to run a million laps around the track on a hot September afternoon, you want a little more encouragement than "C'mon, gang, you can do it!" Maybe something on the order of "C'mon, gang, if you do it I'll let you lie in the grass for the rest of gym period!" would be helpful.

But Mrs. Brockler never seemed to come up with that kind of rallying cry. As we all thudded sweatily around the track, she kept calling out the names of kids who weren't running fast enough.

"C'mon, Gilbert! Pick up those feet!" She meant Mandi Gilbert, who hates running because (she claims) it ruins her pedicure.

"C'mon, Montgomery! Eyes on the prize!" That was addressed to Rad Montgomery, who kept checking out the ice-cream truck parked across the street at the elementary school.

"Good work, Constantin." That was for Voldar, who was so far ahead of the rest of the class that I could hardly see him.

"C'mon, Donohue! Get the lead out of your lingerie!" That was for Brooke.

"*C'mon,* Donohue!" Mrs. Brockler shouted again. "This is gym class, not sleeping class!"

Brilliant line, Mrs. Brockler, I thought as I jogged past her. I noticed she was staring worriedly at someone behind me.

When I threw a glance back over my shoulder, I could see why she was worried. She was watching Brooke. Brooke hadn't just slowed down. She was walking now—and it wasn't even much of a walk. More of a waver, you might say. Her eyes were glassy, her face was leaden gray, and her knees were buckling.

"Brooke? Are you okay?" I asked, turning around and stopping in the middle of the track. Miriam Charney crashed into me. "Roadhog!" she yelled—but I didn't care. I just brushed her aside and ran back to my friend.

As I reached her, Brooke collapsed. I barely managed to catch her on the way down.

"Someone help me get her off the track!" I yelled.

Mrs. Brockler was there in an instant. She lifted Brooke into her arms and carried her gently over to the shade of some nearby bleachers.

"Get some water," she ordered the closest kid. She raced toward the school. The rest of us crowded around Brooke, trying frantically to use up all the oxygen in her vicinity. (Or that's what it looked as if we were doing.)

"Move back," ordered Mrs. Brockler. "Give her some air."

Reluctantly everyone moved about half an inch back except for Miriam Charney, who elbowed her way past me to get a better view.

Brooke tossed her head and moaned. "Get away from me!" she said feverishly.

"See what I mean? Get *back*, gang!" Mrs. Brockler said again.

"Get away, get away," Brooke wailed brokenly. "You'll hurt me. . . ." Her eyes were closed, and her head was whipping back and forth. "You're going to kill me!"

I think we all realized at the same moment that Brooke wasn't talking to us, but to someone inside her head.

"It's okay." Mrs. Brockler tried to soothe her. "We'll have some water for you in a minute."

"*Water is not enough.*" Suddenly Brooke's voice was deep and scratchy. "Blood. A vampire needs fresh blood."

"What's that, Donohue?" Mrs. Brockler sounded startled, and I didn't blame her. She leaned forward and patted Brooke's forehead, but Brooke twisted away.

"Blood," she repeated. "The blood of two people. Three, four, five, six. It's never enough. It's never enough!" Her voice rose to a shriek.

"You bite their necks," she went on in that strange, scratchy voice. Her eyes were open now and fixed up at the sky.

"Ew, grody," said Miriam in disgust.

It's probably not too surprising that when I heard the word *neck*, I looked down at Brooke's. She was wearing a new necklace, I noticed. It was made of a strange, dark metal, and it had a deep red stone in the center.

"Brooke, where did you get that necklace?" I heard myself asking.

At some level Brooke heard me, too. For a split second her eyes opened and stared into mine. She clapped her hand over the jewel in the necklace and wordlessly shook her head.

That stone looked just like the one in Voldar's ring. He had to have given it to her. But why? Just because he wanted to be her friend? Or did the gift give him some kind of ... power over her? Was it helping him turn her into a vampire more quickly?

Was I just imagining things?

Abruptly Brooke began to talk again. "The neck is where the blood flows best, they say," Brooke went on. Then her voice rose. "Thick. Delicious. No! *Don't come near me!* I'll scream! I'll—"

"She's raving." Voldar's voice rose clearly above the confused murmurs of the rest of the class. "I suggest that you take her out of this heat immediately, Mrs. Brockler."

"I think you're right, Constantin," the gym teacher answered. "Let's form a stretcher with our hands, gang. Remember how I showed you last year? Then we can get her to the nurse's office. Lift very, very carefully. Hey, wait! Constantin, what are you doing?"

What Voldar was doing was walking stiffly forward and brushing kids out of his way like scraps of paper. With one swift movement he bent over, scooped Brooke up, and stalked off with her toward the school. Brooke drooped helplessly in his grip, her head lolling back. If I had been in the mood to notice, the two of them would have reminded me of characters in some old movie where the hero rescues the heroine from the train tracks and carries her off into a happy ending.

But all Voldar was doing was carrying Brooke into the nurse's office—and out of earshot.

In her delirium Brooke had been talking about Voldar. I was sure of that.

I was also sure he didn't want to give anything away.

As if I hadn't already had enough fun for one day, the structural engineer came to check out our house that afternoon—a big, bearded, tooloud man named Mr. Brunswick. He had just arrived when I got home from school. When I walked into the kitchen, he was telling my parents that he saw this kind of thing all the time.

"A valve needs tightening somewhere," he suggested. "Or a water pipe needs bleeding. Don't worry, little lady," he added gallantly when he saw me. "We don't *really* bleed the water pipes."

"I didn't think you did," I replied.

"Naturally some families get a little hysterical," Mr. Brunswick went on. He chuckled. "Think there's some kind of ghost in the place!"

"Imagine that," my mother said politely.

"But we generally manage to calm them down. There's a simple scientific explanation for just about everything, you know. Now, where should we start?"

By tearing off your glasses and sailing them around your head like a satellite, our house evidently answered. Because that was exactly what happened. Mr. Brunswick's wire-rimmed glasses toppled off his face and began a lurching zoom around his head.

Mr. Brunswick didn't know what to do. He just stood there, blinking helplessly as his glasses whizzed around and around his head. When the glasses suddenly zipped back onto his nose, he took a wobbly step backward and grabbed the edge of the counter behind him.

"What's the scientific explanation for *that,* Mr. Brunswick?" asked my brother.

"Uh—uh—well, now, naturally I don't know the scientific explanation for *every* phenomenon," Mr. Brunswick answered. "Probably it's some kind of, um, magnetic interference or something. Let's go investigate the rest of the house."

He walked quickly out of the kitchen. After a second the four of us followed him.

"You thought it might be the pipes," Mom reminded him when we were out in the hall. "Would you like to start with them?"

I thought Mr. Brunswick was relieved that someone had made a suggestion—*any* suggestion—about what to do first. "Sure," he said. "Why don't you take me down into the basement so I can look at your heating system?"

Once we were all down there, Mr. Brunswick and my parents got into a long, boring talk about furnaces and stuff. Trevor and I didn't pay much attention, naturally. We started poking around my parents' workbench, straighten-

ing things up and (in Trevor's case) hammering a few nails into the top of the workbench itself. But we both turned around when we heard my mother scream.

Mr. Brunswick was on fire!

Or that's what I thought at first. When I looked more closely, I realized that he was wrapped in a sheet of crackling, silvery fire that was buzzing like a power station. But the flames weren't touching him. To judge by his expression, they weren't even hot.

"Cool!" said Trevor reverently. "A force field!"

Mr. Brunswick was standing motionless, the way some people stand when a bee is crawling on them. "What is it?" he asked in a hushed, terrified voice. "What's happening?"

"I don't know," said my father, his face the color of chalk. "I've never seen anything like it."

As if it was responding to Dad's words, the sheet of flame vanished as quickly as it had come.

Mr. Brunswick drew a shaky breath and wiped his forehead. "Does this happen often?" he asked.

"It never happens," said my mother. "Mr. Brunswick, what on earth do you think could have caused it? You're the expert here."

Now Mr. Brunswick was even more uncomfortable than he'd been up in the kitchen. "Probably the cause is electrical–uh–impulses," he said briefly. "Happens a lot in old houses like this one." He wiped his forehead again. "Maybe I should look up on the second floor now," he suggested. I think he wanted to get as far away from our heating system as possible.

Things didn't improve for poor Mr. Brunswick once he was out of the basement, though. A floor-length curtain in my parents' bedroom reached out and blindfolded him when he went to look out the window. A basketball-size mass of dust rolled out from under the sofa and shot up the chimney. And—I hate to say this, but I shouldn't leave anything out—the toilet flushed whenever Mr. Brunswick walked by the bathroom.

I guess it was Collapsing Day in the town of Litchfield. It didn't take long for Mr. Brunswick to realize that something more than magnetic interference was at work in our house. Fifteen minutes later, he was lying on the living room sofa, my father fanning him anxiously and my mother off getting him a glass of water.

"Never—never—seen anything like this," Mr. Brunswick wheezed, struggling to sit up. "No explanation for—" He took a big gulp of water. "No explanation for this kind of behavior," he said more clearly now.

"No explanation at *all?*" I asked in dismay. "Don't you even have a *guess?*"

Mr. Brunswick straightened his tie. Then he squared his shoulders and looked at each of us.

"I don't want to sound like some weird movie," he said. "But it's obvious to me that something more is going on in your house than a little structural problem." He leaned toward us. As if hypnotized, we all leaned toward *him.*

"I think your house is possessed," Mr. Brunswick said solemnly.

Well, we could have told him that.

"I've never suggested this before," said Mr. Brunswick, "but maybe you should call in some kind of ... exorcist, or something.

"There's nothing I can do for you. Nothing at all."

Chapter Six

"Next year," my science teacher said importantly, "biology!"

He paused for our reactions, but no one in the class said anything.

"Eighth graders study biology," Mr. Fraction explained. (That really is his name. Wouldn't you have expected him to teach math instead of science?) "And what does biology mean?"

Another pause. Another silence on our part. "Uh . . . reproduction?" someone finally asked.

There was a flurry of giggles throughout the room.

"No, no," said Mr. Fraction impatiently. "It means you'll be doing labwork. Actual experiments and studies in an actual laboratory. And to help get you started, we'll be doing lab projects throughout this school year. Beginning today!"

You sure love making announcements, I thought.

Out of habit, I looked over at Brooke. Whenever teachers said anything dumb, Brooke and I liked to raise our eyebrows at each other. Or we had liked to do that in the past, until she got mad at me. Now she didn't meet my glance–she just stared straight ahead.

I noticed uneasily that Brooke was looking paler than ever. There were gray shadows under her eyes, and she was leaning her head against her hand as though she couldn't support it.

"We'll be starting with an experiment on the circulatory system," Mr. Fraction was saying. "Who can tell me what the body's circulation is? Yes, Voldar?"

"Circulation is the movement of blood through the body's blood vessels," said Voldar. "It is induced by the heart's pumping action."

He licked his lips.

"Very good, Voldar!" Mr. Fraction sounded surprised. "And today we'll be studying the circulatory system of worms."

Great, I thought.

"We'll be dividing into pairs," Mr. Fraction went on, "and each pair will receive an earthworm to share."

"To share *how?*" Patty Yurman asked nervously.

"To dissect together," said Mr. Fraction. He continued on, rolling right over the moan of disgust that met this announcement. "Worms are neat. They have five hearts. Let's see. Patty, you can pair up with Mandi, and, Todd, you work with Julie. And, Voldar, your partner is Meg. . . ."

Oh, no. It couldn't be. I *couldn't* have to dissect a worm with Voldar. Life couldn't be that cruel.

But it could. In about ten minutes Mr. Fraction had trotted us down to the biology lab, set us up at different stations, and given each of us a dead worm on a little tray.

"I can't do this," I muttered through clenched teeth the instant Mr. Fraction was out of earshot. "I am *not* going to cut that worm open."

"Too squeamish, Meg?" Voldar asked tauntingly.

I glared at him. “It’s not *squeamish* to hate cutting open dead worms. It’s just—just common sense. Only a ghoul would like to do something like that.”

“Then I must be a ghoul,” remarked Voldar, “for I am looking forward to the assignment. The circulatory system fascinates me.”

I bet it does, you ghoul.

Voldar picked up a razor blade. “Shall I proceed?” he asked.

“Go ahead. It makes no difference to me.” My eyes were squinched shut.

For the next five minutes everything I learned about worms I learned with my eyes closed.

“Ah,” said Voldar in a satisfied tone. “The incision is a success. One, two, three, four, five ... yes, there are the five hearts. Would you like to open your eyes now, Meg?”

I shook my head.

“I shall now dissect one of the hearts,” Voldar went on. And a couple of seconds later, “Once again the incision is a success.”

I balled my hands into fists and pushed my fists against my squinched-shut eyes.

“You know, Meg, in Drazylvonia I learned a way to stimulate the circulatory system in dead animals.” Voldar sounded almost chatty about it.

“Don’t tell me anything more,” I ordered him. “Not one single thing more.”

Voldar continued as if he hadn’t heard me. “The animals do not return to life, but their blood flows in a very lifelike manner. It is not an easy procedure, of course. It requires some dexterity. Perhaps you would now like to watch?”

“No *way!*” I snapped.

"Very well. The loss is yours. Now, I begin by massaging one of the creature's hearts. . . ."

I was plugging my ears again now. I might have stayed sealed up—eyes shut, ears plugged, breath held—for the whole hour, but something caught me unaware. It was a tiny jet of coolish liquid against my cheek.

My eyes flew open just in time to see a miniature geyser of *dead worm blood* fountaining up into the air—and heading straight at my face.

"Voldar, you turn that thing off!" I yelled without thinking. I scrubbed my cheek furiously with my sleeve.

Voldar smiled at me pleasantly as he covered the little tray with his hand. "I am so sorry, Meg. The experiment was more successful than I expected."

"It certainly was," said Mr. Fraction approvingly. He had just come up behind us. "What fascinating results, Voldar! I've never seen anything like this! Would you mind sharing the procedure with the rest of the class?"

"Of course not, sir." Voldar gave one of his courtly little bows. "Shall Meg assist me?"

"Absolutely. She's your lab partner, isn't she?"

"And a very pleasant one," said Voldar. "Meg, perhaps you would hold this razor for me."

My own non-earthworm heart was throbbing with hatred as I slowly took the razor he was holding out to me.

I hated biology. I hated labwork. I hated earthworms. And most of all I hated Voldar.

"I still think it sounds kind of cool," said Trevor wistfully. "Do you remember how to do the experiment? There are a lot of worms out in the backyard."

"No, Trev. I don't remember *anything* about the experiment," I said firmly. "And whoever tries to make me remember it will be very, very sorry."

My brother sighed. "Okay, but you're not being very scientific."

"Oh, you sound like Voldar," I said scornfully. "I didn't tell you about this to get you on *his* side!"

"Well, why did you tell me?" asked Trevor in a reasonable voice.

"Well, because I—because I—" I cleared my throat. "You know, Trevor, I have this awful feeling that Voldar is a vampire."

Quickly I went through all my reasons for thinking so. Voldar's clothes . . . his attraction to Brooke's neck . . . his incredible wall-scaling abilities . . . and just his general *vampirishness.*

"The worst thing is the way Brooke has changed," I finished. "She's getting weirder by the minute."

"Are you kidding?" Trevor said incredulously. "The worst thing is what's happening to our *house!*"

"Well, that's bad, too," I admitted. "But I feel terrible about Brooke. I hate having to stand around and watch while Voldar changes her."

"So why are you standing around and watching?" asked Trevor in a reasonable tone. "Why don't you rescue her?"

"Rescue her?" I repeated.

"You've done it before," Trevor reminded me. "You saved Pittsy." (Pittsy was a girl on Moose Island who had fallen in love with Vincent, my vampire foe.) "And Vaughn." (Vaughn was a baby vampire whom Pittsy and I had devampirized.) "Why can't you get Brooke out of Voldar's murderous clutches? Isn't that a cool expression, ' murderous clutches'? I read it in a detective story. I've been waiting for a good time to use it."

"This is certainly a good time." I sighed. "You're right, Trev. I should do something now. But for some reason it seems harder here than it did on Moose Island."

"I can help," said Trevor eagerly. "Do you want me to find a stake and plunge it through Brooke's heart?"

"Let's hold off on the stake for a few days," I said. "I promise I'll ask you to help me if I need it. But I think that the first thing I should do is try to talk to Brooke again."

If Brooke would talk to *me*.

Chapter Seven

As I walked up the front path toward Brooke's front door, I wondered why her house seemed so different. It looked the same—brick with black shutters, a red door, and an ivy-covered chimney. The lawn was neatly mowed, and a few brightcolored maple leaves had drifted down to punctuate the green with dots of yellow and red. A nice welcoming suburban house, you'd say, and you'd be right.

So why did a feeling of menace hover over everything?

Well, there were no birds in the trees. That was one difference. The trees beside every other house on the block were rustling and twittering with bird activity. Every other lawn on the block had squirrels racing across the grass doing their fall chores—but the Donohue lawn was empty.

And the golden chrysanthemums in the big pot by the front door were shriveled and dead. That was another little touch.

At least Mrs. Donohue seemed normal when she opened the door. "Well, hello, stranger," she said warmly. "My, it's been a long time!"

"That's not my fault, it's your daughter's," I naturally *didn't* answer. Instead I just asked if Brooke was at home.

"She certainly is," said Mrs. Donohue. "She's upstairs doing her homework. I keep telling her she's working too hard. Why, the school year is only a few weeks old, and she's already exhausted!" A line of worry creased Mrs. Donohue's face. "I'm sure she's not feeling well, either. She seems so pale and irritable. I've been wondering if maybe she picked up a bug in Europe. Have you noticed anything strange about her, Meg?"

"I'm—I'm not sure," I lied. There was no point in telling Mrs. Donohue my suspicions about that. "Maybe she's just growing fast or something."

Mrs. Donohue shook her head. "Maybe. We'll have to see, I guess."

"Is Voldar here?" I asked.

"No, Voldar's at the dentist's this afternoon. He says he has a toothache. I hope *he's* all right! I'm sure dental care in Drazylvonia isn't the best."

I was more interested in what an American dentist would think of Voldar's pointed teeth, but I didn't say that out loud either. I just asked if I could go up and see Brooke.

"By all means, dear. But take it easy. I don't want her getting too tired. Brooke!" she called over her shoulder. "Meg's here!"

There was no answer.

"Brooke! Honey, you have a guest!"

Silence.

"Well, I'm sure she'll be glad to see you," said Mrs. Donohue. "You go right on up."

Suddenly she noticed the pot of dead chrysanthemums by the door. "Oh, for heaven's sake," she said. "That's the third pot that's died on me this week! I wish I knew what I was doing wrong."

I left her clucking over the flowers and walked slowly up the stairs.

Brooke's bedroom door was firmly shut—not very welcoming. I gave a timid knock. (As I've often said, I'm a total coward.)

"Go away, Meg," came Brooke's voice from inside. "I'm studying."

That was an excuse she had never used before. "I'll just take a minute," I said.

I heard a heavy sigh, and then the sound of Brooke dragging herself across the room toward the door. "Well?" she said when she opened it.

Brooke looked absolutely terrible. Maybe she worked harder at looking normal in school and then let things slide when she was at home. Now her shoulders were hunched, her face was gray and lined, her pale mouth was drooping at the corners, her hair hung limp and dull. It was as if someone had—well—drained the life out of her.

"What do you want?" she asked, her voice hoarse.

"Brooke, this has to stop," I said without thinking. "He's killing you! Won't you let me help?"

Brooke gave a short, mirthless laugh. "Help him kill me?"

"No, of course not. You know what I mean."

"No, I don't," said Brooke coldly. "And if you've come to tell me something about Voldar, I don't want to hear it."

So you're starting to suspect him yourself. . . .

"I know I'm driving you crazy," I said, "but I—"

"You sure are," Brooke said. "You don't know the first thing about my life, and you come barging in here to straighten me out! Why wouldn't that drive me crazy?"

"I'm not trying to straighten you out," I said carefully. "I just want to help."

"You want to know the biggest help you could give me right now, Meg? Just get out of my life."

I opened my mouth to answer, but Brooke cut me off.

"I mean it. Stay away from me and Voldar. I'm telling you this for your own good."

And she closed the door in my face.

I waited for a second, then slowly turned away. There was no point in trying again.

As I started back downstairs, I noticed the guest room at the end of the hall. It was Voldar's room now, of course, which explained why there was a Drazylvonian flag on the door. The door was open a crack, and I could just see into the room's murky interior.

I tiptoed quickly down the hall. It wasn't snooping, really. More of a search for incriminating evidence. Anyway, I was practically a member of the family—certainly more of one than Voldar was. And I might have—yes, come to think of it, I *had* left something in here the last time I had visited. A pen, maybe, or a book. Something I needed so badly that I had no choice but to go in and look for it.

The door swung open silently at my touch, and I stepped into Voldar's room.

It certainly wasn't like the guest room I remembered.

The pretty quilted bedspreads still covered the twin beds, and the ruffled curtains still hung at the windows. But they were the only touch of—well—*niceness* in the room. Everywhere, everywhere were little touches that Voldar had added to make the place more homey. Homey according to *his* point of view, I mean.

A jar of dead flowers on the bedside table, next to a gloomy photograph of an ancient, crumbling castle. A snakeskin hanging over the curtain rod. Some kind of revolting experiment-in-progress on the desk—I turned my eyes away quickly. An empty glass with traces of red around the rim. (Piles of dirty clothes everywhere, too, but those were what I would have expected in the room of any guy Voldar's age.)

I didn't see anything that could actually prove Voldar was a vampire. On the other hand, I didn't see anything that could actually prove he was normal. Still, I'd need real evidence to incriminate him. Maybe there was something in his desk....

I tiptoed across the room and swiftly began pulling out the desk drawers. Old homework assignments in the top drawer. Notebooks in the second drawer, all filled with Drazylvonian handwriting. A little iron box in the third drawer. I opened it and found a pile of–dirt.

Dirt? Who kept dirt in a desk drawer?

I stared down at the box, my mind ticking like the timer on a bomb. Vampires, I knew, needed to sleep in the dirt they'd been buried in. Vincent Graver, the first vampire I had ever tangled with, had actually lined his coffin with dirt. Wherever the dirt was, there the vampires had to be; they could never get too far away from it.

Perhaps this handful of earth was from Voldar's coffin. Did he sprinkle it over his sheets at night? Or was it enough to have it close by? Was–

"What are you doing in my room?" came a growl from behind me.

Horrified, I turned to see Voldar glaring at me from the doorway. "Oh, hi," I said faintly. *I have to get away before Brooke and her mother realize I'm in here!* "I was just, uh, putting this away."

"After taking it out, I see." Voldar's voice was indescribably grim. He took a step toward me, and then another. Now I could see that he was shaking with rage.

I couldn't let him get too close. I flung the box of dirt across the room. Dirt showered everywhere as the box clattered across the floor and came to rest under the bed.

With a strangled yell of fury, Voldar vaulted across the room in one bound and began scooping up the dirt with his hands.

This was my chance. I bolted out of the room, dashed down the stairs, and pushed my way past a startled Mrs. Donohue and out the front door. "Thanks! Bye!" I called back to her as I raced out of the house.

I never wanted to see that house, or Voldar, again. All I wanted to do was get away.

But when I got back home—having run all the way—I started to feel guilty. No matter *what* I suspected about Voldar, it had been wrong of me to snoop around in his room. I hated to admit it, but I owed him an apology. And the more I tried *not* to admit it, the more my conscience bothered me.

At first I thought about calling Voldar to apologize. Then I realized that if I went back to the Donohues' house, I might spot some more incriminating clues. In other words, I'd be able to satisfy my conscience *and* my curiosity.

I set out down the street before I could change my mind.

When I got to the Donohues', the house was quiet, and Mrs. Donohue's car was no longer parked in the driveway. Had they all gone out? I glanced up at Brooke's room. . . .

And froze in horror at what I saw inside.

Though the sun was only starting to set, Brooke's window shade was already pulled down. Behind it, in silhouette, I could see the figures of Brooke and Voldar.

He was bending toward her. Brooke was trying to pull away, but Voldar's hands were gripping her shoulders too

tightly. He pulled her closer—closer—and slowly lowered his head toward her neck.

At that moment a huge black bat, the biggest I had ever seen, came swooping down from out of nowhere. With a thin shriek, it launched itself at my face. I could hear its wings pounding and feel the draft as it approached. I could see its glittering, furious eyes, and its deadly sharp teeth that were about to tear my flesh. . . .

"NO!" I screamed at the top of my lungs.

And I tore off down the block faster than I had ever run in my life.

Chapter Eight

I was lost in the park in the middle of the night. Frantically I stumbled through the playground, trying to find an exit, but it had mysteriously disappeared. *They must have closed it because they were afraid little kids would wander into the street*, I told myself.

Still, there had to be a way out. I found it and made my way cautiously down the hill toward a concession stand. Maybe, just maybe, it was still open. Someone there might be able to help me get home. As long as they didn't ask me how I'd gotten here, because I couldn't remember that at all....

The concession stand was open. "Thank goodness," I said, running toward the lights. The person in the booth had his back toward me. "Excuse me. I'm lost," I started to call out–

The words froze in my throat.

It wasn't a person in the concession stand. It was a bat.

And it was huger than any bat I could have imagined. Ten feet tall, at least. With claws as big as my whole hand, and gleaming fangs, and–as I watched in terror–wings that spread out, out, out, and then covered me as the bat flew out of the concession stand, picked me up, and lifted me high above the town. I couldn't decide which was worse: the possibility that he might drop me, or the possibility that he wouldn't. . . .

Then I woke up in my own bed. I was sweating and shaking. I was also furious. This poltergeist-vampire-whatever could do what he wanted to our house, but I didn't want him messing around inside my brain. *I can give myself my own bad dreams,* I thought. *I don't need any stupid poltergeist's help.*

It was time for me to get rid of the poltergeist myself.

" 'Electronic Motors and Generators,' " I murmured to myself. " 'Enclosures.' "

"What are enclosures?" Trevor asked.

"I don't know. 'Entertainers. Estate Liquidators. Excavating Contractors. Exercising Equipment. Exporters . . .' "

I closed the telephone book with a sigh. As if it were mocking me, it began flapping back and forth on the coffee table like a huge fish I had just landed. Across the room the hands on our grandfather clock spun wildly around and around while an invisible hand painted bloody pictures on the walls and a blue flame lapped at the baseboards. In other words, it was an afternoon like any other in the Swain household.

"No listing for exorcists," I told Trevor with a sigh. "I told you there wouldn't be anything in the Yellow Pages. There can't be much of a market for exorcists in Delaware."

"But *now* how are we going to find one?" Trevor said. All I could do was shake my head.

It was a few days after my disastrous visit to Brooke's house. Mom was working at the hospital, and Dad was at an all-day meeting. So, for a few hours, Trevor and I had the house—the noisy, banging, flapping, treacherous house—all to ourselves. In other words, this was the perfect time to find an exorcist.

Maybe I couldn't do anything about Brooke, but I could at least *try* to fix things for my family. If I could find someone to get the poltergeist out of our house, it would be a big help.

But it seemed that that was a big *if*.

"Maybe there's another place to look," Trevor suggested. "What was that word Dad used? When all this started happening? The thing he said some people might say was in our house?"

"I don't know what you—Oh, poltergeist."

"Yeah! Try that!"

I shrugged and turned to the *P's*. For the fourth time all I saw were ads for things I didn't need—Podiatrists, Pollution Control Systems, Pony Breeders . . .

Without warning the words on the page began to move. As if they had suddenly become liquid and someone was stirring them, they swirled around and around before my eyes, forming and re-forming words, growing and shrinking—

"Trevor, come here," I whispered.

Trevor ran over and sat down next to me on the sofa. He got there just in time to see the writing on page 847 rearrange itself one more time and stop moving.

Now, in the very center of the page, there was the tiniest possible line of type.

POLTERGEIST PROBLEMS? CALL MINERVA AT 555-4884.

We stared at each other in amazement. "Well," Trevor said at last, "what are you waiting for? Better call her quickly before the page goes back to normal."

I copied the number before it could disappear. Then, my hands shaking, I reached for the phone.

"Minerva" was a small, dark-eyed dumpling of a woman, and I was positive she was a fake. Surely no *real* exorcist wore so much blue eye shadow, such heavy perfume, so many veils and bracelets and clanking necklaces. She looked as though she had just won a ten-minute shopping spree in a gypsy camp. When I answered the door and saw her, I was glad my parents were away. They would not have appreciated my bringing someone like this into the house.

"You must be Trevor," she greeted me in a throbbing, velvety voice. "I'm delighted to—"

"No, that's my brother," I answered. "I'm Meg."

"Of course! Silly me. I read the vibrations wrong. It could happen to anyone. And I? I am Minerva." She reached out and pressed my limp hand between both of hers. "May I come in?"

"I—Sure," I said weakly and led her inside.

"Now *this*, I know, is Trevor." Minerva's voice was triumphant as she pointed at my brother, who was reading an old issue of *Mad* magazine at the kitchen table.

Very impressive. "Yes, that's Trevor," I replied. "Trev, this is Minerva."

Trevor held out his hand uncertainly—and seemed startled when Minerva turned it over instead of shaking it.

"I shall read your palm, child," she announced. "I feel your aura very strongly."

Trevor looked impressed. "Cool! Really?" he asked. "What does it feel like?"

Minerva did not reply. She was staring down at Trevor's palm.

"Television," she said slowly. "You are very fond of television."

I rolled my eyes toward the ceiling. *That* wasn't much of a reach. All kids Trevor's age are fond of television, aren't they?

But my brother was even more impressed than before. "Yes, that's right!" he exclaimed. "Can you tell me what my favorite show is?"

" 'Late-Night News Update,' " Minerva answered promptly.

Now Trev looked a little disappointed. "Well, uh, not exactly. But you're kind of close. I mean, my favorite show does have an *L* in one of the words. It's—"

"Birds," Minerva interrupted, still staring at Trevor's palm. "Birds are important to you."

Now *that* was a little more surprising. The past summer, birds had been Trevor's main interest. He had spent hours trying to identify them in the woods.

"That's right!" he gasped. "Birds *are* very important to me!"

"No, they're not," Minerva contradicted him.

Trevor's face fell. "They're—they're not?"

"Not anymore," Minerva answered. "At least, you will soon become interested in another subject. And that topic will drive birds out of your head for years."

"What's the subject?" Trevor asked uncertainly.

"Collecting ketchup bottles," Minerva said. "Yes, that is definitely in your future. Many, many, many ketchup bottles."

"*Ketchup bottles!*" Trevor repeated in amazement. "That's so weird! I don't care about them at all now!"

"The future never lies, child," said Minerva. And she gave him back his hand, if you know what I mean.

Well, we'd see about ketchup bottles. Right then I wanted to find out if Minerva could possibly be any use with poltergeists. I kind of doubted it—but as long as she was here, I decided to put her to work.

Right on cue the burners on the stove flared up. The paper towels began to unwind from their dispenser and curl across the kitchen counter. And the faucet started spitting out blasts of horrible brownish water.

"My word! What's the matter?" asked Minerva, growing pale.

"That's what we want you to help us with," I blared above the noise of the faucets. "What do *you* think is the matter?"

"It—it's hard for me to concentrate with all this noise," Minerva replied piteously. "Perhaps we could investigate the rest of the house?"

I shrugged. "Sure," I said and led her and Trevor into the living room.

The house was lively that day, just the way it had been when the structural engineer had visited. And just as he hadn't really known what to tell us, Minerva didn't, either. She grew paler and paler as we marched upstairs and bottles of cough syrup spilled themselves on the bathroom floor ... as the bed in my room rapidly made and unmade itself ... as a lipstick wrote DEATH TO MINERVA on my mother's dressing table mirror. (Well, that would have scared me, too.) But she didn't have much to say.

"This is intensely cosmic," she murmured at one point.

"Very noticeable vibrations here," she said in our spare room (where a huge chasm had appeared in the floor and swallowed up a chair).

"Fascinating," she managed to whisper when a cleaver sliced through the air just inches in front of our faces. "Extremely—fascinating."

"So what's your diagnosis?" I asked abruptly when we'd shown her every room in the house. I knew Mom and Dad would be back soon, and I didn't want them to find her here. "What's doing this to us? And why?"

Minerva took a deep breath. (A pen cap that had been magically whizzing through the air got sucked into her mouth, but luckily she spat it out before it choked her.) "Someone is angry with you," she said.

"Yes, I figured that," I said coolly.

"And, uh—this someone is quite, quite furious."

"Um-hmmmm," I said.

"I'm sensing"—I thought Minerva looked a little panicky now—"that this is a being with whom someone in your family has done battle in the past. Now the being wants revenge."

"Cool!" piped up Trevor, who still hadn't realized that Minerva was a phony. "What kind of being is it?"

Minerva looked puzzled. "Well, it's not a ghost," she finally said. "I'm getting that quite clearly. It's some other kind of spirit. I'm sensing that it's a—

"*VAAMMMMMMPIIIIIIIIIIIRE,*" she suddenly bellowed out in a deep, hollow voice.

The voice was like a blast in a tunnel. Trevor and I practically fell over backward, we were so startled.

And then, for the second time that day, a familiar surface began to change form in front of my astonished eyes. Only this time it wasn't a page in the phone book. It was Minerva's face.

Her skin began to twist and bubble and churn, like clay being kneaded by invisible hands. It grew pale, pale, paler—

as pale as death. Her eyes widened, lengthened, and sank deep into her head. Her nose jutted out over a thinning mouth.

"Meg, what's happening?" Trevor sounded as though he were about to cry. He slipped his hand into mine.

"I don't know," I whispered.

Now Minerva opened her mouth in a silent scream, so wide I could hear her joints cracking. Her teeth, I saw, were turning pointed.

Pointed teeth! As though she were becoming a—

"A vampire," Trevor whimpered, and I knew his thoughts had been running in the same direction as mine.

Yes. That was what Minerva's face had become: a vampire's face. The body was just the same, the clothes were just the same, and the face was that of a vampire.

Not just any vampire's, either. This was a face I knew all too well. When he spoke to me, I recognized the voice right away.

"So we meet again, Meg," he growled.

My heart was gripped with icy fear, but I couldn't let Trevor know that. I was supposed to be taking care of him, after all.

So I was proud of how calmly I answered.

"Yes, Vincent," I replied. "Indeed we do."

Chapter Nine

Minerva—or should I still call her Minerva?— was leaning rigid against the wall. The deep voice pouring out of her throat seemed to have no connection to her body. Nor did Vincent's face—wreathed by Minerva's frizzy hair—appear to have anything to do with Minerva. In any other circumstances the sight might have been funny. But I knew, and Trevor knew, that it was dead serious.

Vincent spoke again. "This is only the beginning, Meg," he said. "Only the beginning of what lies in store for you. You have not seen half my wrath yet."

"Wrath?" Again, for Trevor's sake, I tried to sound cocky. I didn't want my brother to be more scared than he absolutely had to be. "You call sticking your face onto Minerva's body *wrath*? Remind me to look up *wrath* in the dictionary sometime."

"I am not speaking of this visitation, Meg," growled Vincent. "I refer to my taking up residence in your home. You have, no doubt, observed some strange occurrences recently."

"That was you?" I asked impudently. "You're the one who fried the eggs on the kitchen floor? Whew! Scared me to death! You know what might *really* scare me? If you left a banana peel on the ground, and I stepped on—"

"Silence, Meg!" thundered Vincent.

"Don't get him mad, Meg," whispered Trevor at the same time.

"You would be wise, as usual, to listen to your brother," said Vincent. "He has a proper sense of respect for me—respect that you appear to lack."

"Okay. I'll try to control myself. But, Vincent, even you have to admit that taking over some woman's face and throwing pen caps around doesn't seem like first-class scare tactics. Why couldn't you try a little harder?"

"I must use the resources available to me," said Vincent coldly. "This medium—this Minerva—is a rather foolish specimen, I admit. However, she is at least partially psychic, and I can only reappear through a psychic medium. As far as the activities in your home . . . well, give me credit for improving my technique. Possessing an entire house takes a great deal of energy, and I am only now beginning to hone my skills. The cleaver I hurled at you, for instance, is a definite improvement over the fried eggs."

There was a silence while I digested this. "Well, that's true," I admitted at last. "The cleaver was pretty good. Actually, you *have* been getting better lately." And even though I wasn't admitting it, seeing Vincent's face on Minerva's head was becoming more off-putting by the second.

"But, Vincent, why are you doing all this?" I went on. "Because believe me, I'd be just as glad if you'd spare yourself the trouble."

"The reason is simple," said Vincent. "Revenge. I will never give up trying to destroy your life."

I took a deep breath. Yes, that was simple enough.

"You ruined mine," Vincent added. "You took away every chance I had to exist in my own body. You made it impossible for me to return to earth as myself. Never, never again will I walk the stony paths of my native land. Never again will I know the pleasure of drinking fresh blood. Never again will I have the chance to tear apart a throbbing, still-warm—"

"I get the idea," I interrupted hastily. "You're mad at me."

"That would be the mildest way of putting it."

"Well, Vincent, before you destroy my life, can I ask you a few questions? This may be our only chance to talk again." To my surprise, I felt the tiniest pang of regret at the thought. "If you're going to destroy me, I want to understand as much as I can about how you're doing it."

"Ask, and I will try to answer."

"First of all, who is Voldar?"

Silence.

"Voldar?" repeated Vincent. "I do not know this name."

"But he's—yes, you do! You have to!" I protested. "I'm sure he's a vampire. He's going to my school this term. He's from Drazylvonia, and he has pointed teeth, and—"

"I do not know him," Vincent repeated, "though I have relatives in Drazylvonia. If this Voldar were a vampire, I would have heard of him."

I stood silently for a minute, digesting this. If what Vincent said was true—and although he was my worst nightmare, I had never known him actually to lie—that meant Brooke was in no danger from Voldar. What, then, would explain the changes in her?

"Are *you* vampirizing my friend Brooke?" I suddenly asked.

"Detestable word, *vampirizing,*" said Vincent-Minerva. "No, I am not preying on your friend. As I have said, I have no more need of earthly sustenance. However, I will add that on the day she visited you, I sensed signs of vampiric possession in her."

"So you're, like, watching us all the time?" I asked.

"I am," Vincent replied.

"*All* the time?" Trevor repeated.

Was it my imagination or did the ghost (excuse me) of a smile enter Vincent's voice at that point? "I allow privacy at the appropriate moments," he said.

"Thanks," said Trevor.

"But back to you, Vincent," I said. "Basically, you just stopped in to warn me that this is a fight to the death. Is that right?"

"I 'stopped in,' as you put it, because the opportunity to do so—via this medium—was there for me. I do not know if I will ever contact you again. But I was, of course, delighted to have the chance to warn you of your fate."

"Thanks a lot," I said bleakly. "I appreciate it."

"And now I will take my leave of you," said Vincent. "I have told you enough."

His voice was becoming thinner, I realized—thinner and farther away. "Wait!" I begged. "Can't you tell me just—"

"No more, Meg." The voice was dying away. "You have been warned. . . ."

Minerva shuddered. As we watched, her face twisted itself back to its normal shape. She blinked rapidly several times, and then she finally stopped, her eyes were her own again. She shook her head dazedly, and the last traces of Vincent disappeared from sight.

"Wha' hap–?" she croaked. She cleared her throat and tried again. "What happened?" she managed to say this time.

I put a hand on her shoulder. "You were–uh–taken possession of."

"*Vampiric* possession," Trevor added proudly. "That's what Vincent calls it."

"Vincent?" Minerva repeated in a faint voice. "Who is Vincent?" She rubbed her eyes with a limp hand, smearing blue eyeshadow all over her forehead.

"He's a–he's a–well, never mind," I said. "Let's just call him a spirit you called up."

Minerva's jaw dropped. "*I* channeled a *spirit?*" she gasped. "Oh, that's marvelous! I've never been able to–"

She stopped and cleared her throat. "Of course, channeling will cost you extra," she said primly.

I didn't argue. I was sure Minerva had never called up a spirit before, and I was equally sure she would never do it again. But the fact that she had done it this time was worth a lot to me.

At least now I knew what I was up against.

Not that I had the faintest idea how to fight against a vampire I couldn't even see.

When I had paid Minerva (luckily I had a lot of money stashed in the top drawer of my bureau) and sent her on her way, Trevor and I collapsed onto the living room sofa.

Trevor looked white and sick. "What are we going to do, Meg?" he asked. "I mean, if he's *everywhere* ... are we breathing him right now, do you think?"

"I don't know," I answered wearily. "If we are, maybe that's the reason my hay fever has been so bad this year. Maybe I'm allergic to Vincent-dust."

"He said he was getting better with practice," Trevor reminded me. "So what do you think that means?"

I didn't want to tell him, but I was sure it meant the worst. Vincent wasn't the kind of person—vampire, I mean—to go back on his word. If he was out to destroy me (whatever he meant by that), there was no reason to think he wouldn't accomplish what he had set out to do.

It isn't exactly fun walking around with the threat of destruction over your head.

What was I going to do?

What was I going to do?

Chapter Ten

"No, thanks," said Brooke wearily. "I don't feel like it."

"Oh, come on," I begged. "You haven't spent the night here in ages. Not since you came back from France! And I'd really like to have your company."

Mom and Dad were going out to dinner that Friday night—some kind of business thing they couldn't get out of. I had decided to use the time to talk to Brooke. It was my best chance to find out what was the matter with her. Now that I knew Vincent was back, I was getting really worried. About Brooke, about my house, about everything. I couldn't figure out how to deal with Vincent, but at least maybe I could help Brooke somehow.

"You'll have Trevor," Brooke pointed out. "And the cat."

"Oh, come on, Brooke. They're not as much fun as you are." *Or as you used to be, anyway,* I thought.

There was a long, long pause.

"Well, I have to check with my mother," Brooke said at last. "She may have other plans for me. Maybe we have to take Voldar to a concert or something that night," she added hopefully. "Hang on a sec."

Brooke was gone a long time—so long that I was sure she was having a fight with her mother. When she finally picked up the phone again, she sounded gloomier than before. "Mom says it would be fine," she reported. "She thinks it would be good for me to get out of the house. What time do I have to—I mean, what time would you like me to come over?"

"How about coming home on the bus with me on Friday?" I asked.

There was another pause. "No. I'll need to walk home with Voldar," Brooke said. "I'll come over in time for supper."

"Great," I said fervently. "Fantastic." My enthusiasm must have sounded strange to Brooke, who'd made it so clear she didn't want to come.

That was on a Tuesday. For the rest of the week Vincent kept his poltergeist activities to a minimum. I don't know why. Maybe he wanted to lull me into a false sense of security, or maybe he was just tired out from the strain of appearing through Minerva's body. Anyway, things got a lot calmer.

"The only thing I was worried about was leaving you guys alone tonight if the house got really kooky," Mom said happily at breakfast. "And now I don't even have to worry about that. Whatever was the matter is obviously all fixed. I bet we won't have any more trouble."

As we all know, mothers are terrible at predicting the future.

Mom and Dad had already left before Brooke finally dragged herself over to our house that night. She looked even sicker than the last time I had seen her. (Once again I had to give her credit for a great acting job. If she felt this bad all the time, she was doing an excellent job of hiding it at school.) If my parents had realized what kind of shape

Brooke was in, they would never have left home so cheerfully.

"Hi," Brooke said listlessly, shuffling through the fallen leaves on the front walk. "How're you?"

"I'm okay, I guess. But you're not, Brooke. What's the matter? You're looking awfully tired these days." "Washed out" was what I didn't want to say.

Brooke pulled her duffel bag up the front steps (it took all her strength, I noticed) and dumped it inside the front hall. Then she staggered into the living room and dropped into an armchair.

"I *am* tired," she confessed. "Tired of everything. Sometimes I—I wish I could just go to sleep and never wake up." A single tear slowly trickled down her pale cheek.

"Brooke, why?" I asked. "Is it something to do with Voldar?"

At that, she sat straight up. "No. Why should it be?" she asked sharply.

"No reason," I said. "I was just wondering. I mean, you seem to have started—well, you know—changing once he came to stay."

"Voldar has nothing to do with this!" Brooke snapped. "I don't know why you're so suspicious of him, Meg. He's never done anything to you, has he?"

"No," I admitted. "He hasn't." And suddenly I was filled with guilt.

Here I was suspecting Voldar of trying to hurt Brooke when I had *knowingly* invited her to a house possessed by a vampire. I had brought her to this horribly dangerous spot on purpose. I'd wanted to help her, but wasn't I kidding myself? If you want to help someone, you don't treat them like vampire bait!

"Now *you* look weird," Brooke said. "What's the matter?"

"Brooke, I—I have to confess something. I hope you won't hate me when I tell you."

And I told her everything about Vincent Graver.

How he had started out as our babysitter. How we had realized what he *really* was. How my friend Jack and I had gotten rid of him—or thought we had.

How Vincent had come back the following summer. How I had found his ring, with its strange powers.

When she heard about the ring, Brooke clapped a protective hand over her necklace. "They sound almost identical, the ring and this necklace," she said breathlessly. "Voldar gave me this. He brought it from home."

"I figured," I said dryly.

I went on with my story about Vincent. What had happened the previous summer, while Brooke was away in France. How Minerva had channeled Vincent, whether she had meant to or not.

And what Vincent had told me about taking possession of my house. How he was lurking, waiting for me at that very moment.

How I'd begged her to come spend the night, knowing all the time that I was asking her to keep me company in a—"Well, practically a haunted house," I finished uncomfortably. "I'm really sorry, Brooke. It was totally selfish of me. I'm sure you'll want to go home now, and I don't blame you."

"No, of course I don't want to go home. In fact, there's something I should tell you. I've been a real coward about it." Brooke paused, biting her lip.

"Well?" I prompted her.

Right at that moment the floor shook slightly under my feet. For a second I thought I heard that strange, demonic cackle. Brooke looked even more startled than I felt.

"It's a little complicated," she said. Then, abruptly, "I guess it's *too* complicated. Forget it. Let's just watch some TV."

For the rest of the evening, I could tell that Brooke was trying to be a good guest. She had to work at it, but she *did* do her best. We watched a little TV (Brooke kept dropping off to sleep, but then, it was a pretty boring show), and then we told Trevor we would make him whatever he wanted for supper. Brooke helped me cook Trev's "meal." (Ten pieces of bacon and, for dessert, a bag of chocolate chips.) Then we watched a bunch more TV, and then we ordered in a pizza (Brooke said it smelled good, but she wouldn't eat any of it) and watched more TV. It wasn't lots and lots of fun, but it was okay. Almost normal, in fact.

So you'll understand why it came as a shock when I woke in the middle of the night and found myself alone in my room, frozen to my bed by some sinister force. And Brooke was gone.

Chapter Eleven

When I say I was frozen to my bed, I don't mean literally frozen. I mean paralyzed.

At first I thought that somehow the covers had gotten too tight while I was sleeping. But the more I thrashed around trying to loosen them, the tighter they seemed to become. It took no more than a couple of minutes before I couldn't move at all. I was trapped inside a bed that had gone as hard as marble.

All around me a thick, evil red vapor swirled, turning the room into a hellish nightmare. Nothing looked the way it usually did, and I couldn't see Brooke's bed at all.

"Brooke?" I called in a half-whisper.

When she didn't reply, I spoke more loudly. Then louder, and louder still. Still there was no answer from her side of the room.

I paused for a moment, listening. If Brooke was asleep, shouldn't I be able to hear her breathing? Then why couldn't I hear anything at all?

I strained desperately to see the other bed. Finally I was able to wrench myself up on my elbows for an instant. It was only an instant—but it was enough to make it clear that there was no one sleeping in Brooke's bed.

A faint, faint whisper floated through the air, so faint that at first I thought I was dreaming.

"Don't let her move," the hushed voice murmured. "Keep her there."

There was an answering murmur of agreement, and I felt hands as cold and strong as iron clasping my shoulders and pressing me down.

Now stealthy footsteps were approaching my bed. For the first time I knew what it meant to be too frightened to scream.

Closer and closer came the steps. "Get her ready," the quiet voice whispered.

One of the hands holding me shifted its position and grasped my chin, tilting it back so my neck arched upward. "She is ready," someone muttered.

Now I knew what was going to happen.

The air around me turned even colder as the stranger approached. Then another pair of hands—smaller than the first pair but just as cold—pinned my wrists to the bed. I heard someone breathing now, and the breathing was coming closer.

Suddenly two red-glowing eyes beamed through that thick darkness, bringing a faint light to the room—and I saw that they were Brooke's eyes, murderously fixed on my neck.

Brooke was the vampire.

No flicker of life nor trace of recognition could be seen in her eyes' dead red glare. They lit up her white face with its skull-like shadows and her gleaming teeth, teeth that were now only inches from my neck....

The only sound I could make was a terrified whimper. I watched helplessly, hopelessly, as those pointed teeth came closer and closer.

But when I actually felt the two sharp pricks on my skin, something inside me wrenched itself free. With all my strength I twisted my chin free and gasped, "*Brooke!* No! Please don't do this!"

She froze and lifted her head for a second. "Don't make this difficult, Meg," she said dully.

"Don't make it *difficult!*" I said indignantly. "Why shouldn't I make it difficult for you to turn me into a *vampire?*"

"You won't turn into a vampire," Brooke answered. "It takes three bites to turn someone into a vampire—you know that. All I'm asking for is one. One little bite. You can do me this favor." Her voice sharpened. "I have to have blood to live, Meg. I *need* it. Please!"

"Wait a minute. Wait a minute," I begged. "Can we just back off for a sec? Don't I—don't I get to ask a few questions first? I mean, we were supposed to be best friends."

Brooke sighed and straightened up. "That's true." She spoke to her invisible companion. "Let her go for now, Vincent. We can catch her again in a minute."

The red vapor thinned out a bit. The hands holding me down relaxed their grip. The bedcovers loosened, and I could move again. Not far enough to get away, though—I was sure of that.

"Meg, I'm a vampire now. I don't have time for friends." Brooke's voice was bleak. "You of all people should understand what that's like. All I think about is blood, blood, blood. And where do you find blood in a place like Litchfield? What are you supposed to do, walk up to people you know—people you've grown up with—and ask them for a blood donation? I just haven't been able to do it. But now I'm too weak to hold out any longer."

"When did this all start?" I asked, hoping that I *could* make her hold out a little longer.

"When I was in France," Brooke answered. "Or not in France, really. The family I was living with took me on a vacation to Drazylvonia. We stayed in this little farmhouse at the edge of some woods. . . ." Her voice trailed off, and she shuddered.

"There were bats in the farmhouse. Living in the attic. And my room was right next to the attic. One night a bat got into my room and bit me while I was sleeping. It bit me three times—we found three sets of marks in the morning."

"Why didn't you wake up?" I asked blankly.

Brooke shook her head. "I don't know. I'd been out hiking that day, and I was tired. Or maybe the bat bit me very gently. There are some kinds of vampire bats that anesthetize you when they bite—I've read about them. Anyway, it happened.

"And besides, it wasn't a real bat. The next thing we heard was that this madman dressed all in black had been caught in the village at midnight, trying to drink blood from a horse. He claimed he was a vampire and that he had already bitten half the people in town by turning himself into a bat and creeping into their houses—" Her voice broke.

"Naturally the authorities didn't believe him. They packed him off to an asylum somewhere—they're pretty old-fashioned about those things in these little villages, I guess. And a couple of days after that we left town. I never did find out whether other people in the town had actually become vampires. I suppose *they've* found out by now."

"So when did you figure out that it had happened to you?" I asked.

"Not for a while. When we were back in France, I started having nightmares and getting weaker and weaker. Then one day a mosquito bit me, and I knew."

"How?"

"I licked the bite to get the blood," Brooke said simply. "The second that taste was in my mouth, I felt as if my whole body were on fire. I had never tasted anything I wanted so much. And I realized what I had turned into."

"What did you do?" I whispered.

"I started reading," Brooke said grimly. "I found out everything I could about vampires. And the main thing I found out was that the more blood I drank, the more of a vampire I would be. Every drop of someone else's blood changes your body a little bit more.

"So I decided that maybe I could keep it under control. You know—not get too vampirish. I figured that if I changed the way I dressed, people might not notice the other changes in me. Black clothes make people look paler anyway, so I thought that you'd all think I looked pale because of what I was wearing. And I hoped that maybe once I was back home, I wouldn't be so tempted to—to bite."

"I guess it didn't work," I said sadly.

Brooke shook her head. "Until now it hasn't been too bad. I was managing. And I thought that if things got really hard—well, there was always Voldar. He wouldn't be staying in the U.S. too long, so maybe I wouldn't have to hurt him too badly."

"So Voldar's not a vampire?" It was hard for me to accept that. I could see I'd gone way, way overboard in my judgment of Voldar. But he had seemed like such an obvious suspect!

"No. Voldar's not a vampire." Brooke smiled a little. "He just looks like one. I *like* the way he looks, though," she added quickly. "I really like him a lot. I—I more than like him. I guess that's why the couple of times I've wanted to bite him, I've been able to hold off."

I suddenly remembered the scene I had watched through Brooke's window and told her what I had seen. "I thought he was trying to bite you," I confessed.

Brooke let out a dry little chuckle. "No, my necklace—that necklace he gave me—had gotten caught in one of his collar buttons. We were just trying to get it untangled. And it was so hard for me not to bite him then!"

"Well, you don't feel the same way about me, so naturally you can't hold off *now*," I said bitterly.

"But, Meg, I've been trying so hard," Brooke's voice quavered. "Why do you think I've been so snotty to you? I thought I could, you know, drive you away from me, and then at least *you* would be safe! That's why I said I didn't want to come over. I've been getting so weak that I didn't know if I could trust myself."

"Why did you suddenly get in a better mood tonight, then?" I asked.

Brooke's face fell. "Oh, I hate to admit this, Meg. But it's because I figured it would help you get to sleep better. You know—because you wouldn't be nervous or anything."

"Ick," I said flatly. "That doesn't really convince me that you're a great friend."

Brooke sighed. "I know. I know it doesn't. But can't you understand what a relief it was for me once I knew I'd be getting some blood, even just one dose? So once you were asleep, I contacted Vincent—"

"How?" I interrupted.

"Simple. I just whispered his name. I was pretty sure he'd be able to talk to me—and he could. And just as I'd guessed, he was happy to help me."

In the dim light I could see her lick her lips. Oh, how could I stall her any longer? There was only one thing I could think of. . . .

"You know, Brooke, I bet I can cure you!" I said excitedly. "I cured the baby from turning into a vampire. I cured Pittsy. I know I can figure out a way to de-vampirize you. There's got to be some way out of this. I'm sure there is!"

There was no answer.

"Brooke? *Brooke?*"

To my horror, Brooke's voice was starting to sound lifeless and dull again. "I'm sure there isn't, Meg. And all that excitement must have drained my energy, or something. When I woke up tonight, I realized that I couldn't wait any longer. I'm glad I got to tell you everything, but I need blood. And I need it *now.*"

She raised her voice and spoke to her invisible companion. "Hold her down. It's time," she said.

Chapter Twelve

I didn't care that it would take three bites before I turned into a full-fledged vampire. I didn't care that I'd be doing my best friend a big favor by letting her sink her teeth into my neck. I just couldn't bear the thought of Brooke biting me. Period.

"Brooke, don't!" I begged frantically. "Just give me one more day!"

"Another day won't make any difference to you," Brooke answered, "and I need blood *now.* I can't wait. I'm sorry, Meg."

"But I think I can help you!" Suddenly an idea sprang into my head. A flimsy idea, but it's not that easy to think of nice substantial ideas when you're fending off a vampire. "I can—I can make a deal to stop this happening to you!" I said.

"Yeah, right. A deal," Brooke answered, mocking me. "A pact with the devil or something? There's no one on earth who can help me."

But I wasn't talking about someone on earth. I was talking about someone who definitely was *not* on earth.

Vincent.

I had talked to him once before. If I could talk to him again, maybe I'd be able to persuade him to help Brooke. Surely between now and then I could come up with some kind of trade to offer him—something in exchange for Brooke's soul? There had to be!

Brooke finally let me talk her into waiting for twenty-four hours, until the next night. "But don't come near me until then," she warned sternly. "I'll stay in the guest room with the door closed. Keep Trevor and your parents away, and you stay away yourself. I can't answer for what will happen if either of you gets too close."

I promised, and she stumbled away into the darkness and down the hall. After a second I heard her close and lock the door.

"Are you there?" I whispered to Vincent.

Silence, of course.

"I know you are," I whispered again. "I know you can hear me. Please, Vincent. I'm begging you. If there's anything you can do to help Brooke, *I'll* do anything to help you. You'll have some time to think about it," I added. "And I'll look forward to hearing from you tomorrow night."

I know it sounded as though I was signing a letter, but that's all I could think of to say.

* * *

By morning I still hadn't figured out how to keep my parents away from the guest room for the next twenty-four hours. But I guess everyone gets saved by the bell once per lifetime, and that morning it was my turn. It wasn't a bell, it was a telephone, but—well—anyway, they both ring, don't they?

"Good morning, honey," Mom said when I came down to breakfast. "Is Brooke still sleeping?"

"Uh—yes. She's really tired. I gave her the guest room. In fact, she's going to be—"

I was going to say, "She's going to be sleeping in there all day," but at that moment the phone rang. Dad answered it and handed it over to Mom. "The hospital," he said.

"Hi," said Mom perkily. *"What?"* she said, less perkily. "What? Tonight? Why? What? *What? Ick!* Okay."

"What was that all about?" my father asked.

"Oh, something's come up at the hospital," Mom said disgustedly. "It's too boring and complicated to explain. But I'm going to go over there around twelve or so, and I won't be back until late tonight. You'll all be okay without me, won't you?"

"Sure!" I started to say happily. But my father spoke right over me.

"I'm going to a screening in Washington tonight. I'll be driving in after lunch. Remember?"

"You never told me about it!" Mom got up to look at the calendar. "And you didn't write it down, either."

"Well, I thought I had. Anyway, I've got to go to this thing," Dad said grumpily. "I'll get a sitter, don't worry."

"Don't *you* worry, Dad. I can sit for Trev again tonight."

"Oh, Meg, I hate for you to have to do that," my mother said unhappily. "You shouldn't have to be responsible two nights in a row. Besides, Dad and I might both get back way too late for you. He'll call around and find someone to take care of Trevor so you can relax."

I *did* relax when Dad couldn't find a single sitter. "I guess I left it until too late," he told me, mussing my hair. "Sorry, Meg. You'll have to be on duty after all."

"It's okay, Dad. It'll make things a lot simpler. Really."

As soon as both my parents were out of the house ("I've never known Brooke to sleep *this* late!" Mom said wonderingly at lunchtime), I went right to the phone and called Minerva.

"Meg Swain?" she said in a faraway voice. "I'm afraid I don't know a Meg Swain."

"You channeled someone's spirit over at my house," I reminded her.

"Oh! *That* Meg Swain!" Suddenly she sounded a lot more interested. "I'm sorry. You see, I've been dealing so intensely with the spirit world that it's hard for me to keep my mind on worldly things."

Yeah, right.

"Anyway, Meg, what can I do for you?"

"I was wondering if you might be able to channel the same spirit again," I said. "I need to get in touch with him right away. He might be able to help a friend of mine. It's very important."

"I would be delighted to help you, child. But remember, I charge extra for channeling," Minerva warned me. "Having a spirit speak through your body is very, very stressful. Why, I might even *collapse* from the stress." She sounded as though she rather enjoyed that idea.

"I'll pay whatever you ask," I said desperately. (There went all the money I had been saving for new skis.) "Can you come tonight?"

Minerva was not psychic enough to remember where my house was—even though she'd been there before. But I hoped that she would be back in form by the time evening came.

When I had finished talking to her, I went upstairs and knocked on Brooke's door. "It's me," I said. "Are you awake?"

There was no answer, and for a panicky moment I wondered if Brooke had actually starved to death in there. But then I heard her faintly calling, "Don't try to come in, Meg. It's not safe."

"I won't," I promised. "I just wanted to tell you what I'm going to try tonight. I know it sounds weird, but ..."

When I had finished explaining everything, I could hear Brooke sigh. "It won't work," she said in a discouraged voice. "Why should Vincent want to do you any favors?"

"I'm hoping he'll let me do one for him in return," I said.

"But what kind of favor can you do for a disembodied vampire?" Brooke said.

And I had to admit I had no idea.

Minerva got to our house at about eight o'clock that night, an hour after she had said she'd be there. She claimed she'd gotten lost on the way.

"I didn't know psychics could get lost," said Trevor with interest. "Why couldn't you just *beam* yourself to our house?"

Minerva eyed him coldly. "You know, I find that having children nearby disturbs my channeling powers," she answered. "I'm afraid that I'll have to ask you to go to bed now, little boy."

"I was here the last time you changed the channels, or whatever you call it," protested Trevor. "Remember how your face looked like gum being chewed? Your cheeks went all sideways and your chin started to—"

"That's enough," snapped Minerva. "I want you asleep before I begin channeling. Is that clear?"

Trevor looked questioningly at me. "Do I have to?"

"I think you'd better, Trev," I said reluctantly. "That is important. Besides, things might get pretty scary."

"But that's why I would *like* being here!" Trevor wailed. "I might get to see Vincent rip out someone's heart or something! Or maybe he'll come bursting out of Minerva's body and—"

"It won't be that exciting, I promise," I said quickly. "It'll just be like last time, only with more talking."

At least I hoped so.

Trevor reluctantly went upstairs—"But you can't stop me from *listening*," he said crossly—and I asked Minerva whether I should bring Brooke downstairs now. "Will you be able to channel that spirit pretty quickly?" I asked. "I don't think Brooke can hold out for much longer."

"By all means bring the girl down immediately," said Minerva grandly. "I have total confidence in my powers."

When Brooke unlocked the guest room door, I was shocked by how pale and wasted she was. She took one step out into the hall and fell to her knees. I bent down to help her up, but she cried out hoarsely, "Don't touch me! Don't come near me!"

So I had to watch as, with agonizing slowness, she dragged herself to her feet again. Leaning against the wall, she inched herself over to the stairs. To get to the banister, she had to pull herself free of the wall, which left her swaying sickeningly at the top of the stairs. For one horrible moment I thought she was going to fall, but at the last second she stretched out a clawlike hand and gripped the banister tightly.

"Okay so far," she said, giving me a weak smile. "And it's all downhill from here."

Please, Vincent. Please help her, I prayed silently. *I can't stand seeing her like this.*

When Brooke had finally limped downstairs and collapsed into a wing chair, I could tell that Minerva was shocked at her appearance, too. "You must be Brooke," she said. "I—I'm glad to meet you, my dear. Well!" she added brightly. "Are we all ready?"

There was a knock at the door.

"Meg!" Trevor called shrilly from upstairs. "There's someone at the door! What's happening? Who is it?"

"Don't worry," I called to him. "It's just–"

"Voldar," said Voldar quietly. He was standing on the front step.

"Voldar!" I echoed in my normal voice. "What–what are you doing here?"

"I came to see Brooke. I was worried about her. She has not been herself recently, and I was hoping that maybe this visit with you had raised her spirits somewhat."

"Good phrase–'raising spirits,' " Brooke said with a croaky chuckle.

Now Voldar noticed her for the first time. "*Brooke!*" he gasped. "What has happened to you?"

Minerva stepped forward quickly. "You don't want to know, dear," she said. "The three of us are going to transact some business here, and it would be best if you didn't see it."

"No, he can stay," said Brooke. "I–I want him to stay."

She gave him a wan smile. "I know you think I'm weird, Voldar," she said. "You're too polite to say it, but I know. Maybe this will help you understand what's been going on with me."

Her voice was starting to fade, and I knew we had no more time. "We'll explain later, Voldar," I said quickly. "Now, Minerva. *Now.*"

"Oh, dear," said Minerva after a second in which nothing happened. "I guess the spirits are off tonight."

"They can't be!" I wanted to shake her. "You've got to get Vincent. You've *got* to!"

Minerva shrugged apologetically. "I wish I could, Meg, but you know how it is. Sometimes, in this life, we just have to face disappointment. I'm a skilled medium, but–

“WHAT DO YOU WANT, MEG?” she suddenly boomed in a deep, echoing bellow.

That was Vincent’s voice! “Vincent!” I said excitedly. “It’s working!”

“What is happening to her?” asked Voldar in horror.

“She’s channeling a vampire,” I explained. I could see why he was startled.

Minerva’s face was stretching and bubbling and turning gray. Her teeth pricked into points, and she gave that horrifying silent scream. Then Vincent’s face emerged from Minerva’s doughy features. He was glaring viciously at me.

“This is a serious imposition, Meg,” he said through Minerva.

“Oh, it is not,” I said crossly. “It’s not nearly as serious as what’s happening to Brooke.” Voldar had crossed the room to stand next to Brooke, and she was leaning her head against Voldar’s shoulder as if the strain of holding it up was too much for her.

“‘I mean the imposition of being forced to make my appearance via this dismal charlatan.”

“You mean Minerva?” I asked.

“Of course. She has the most inferior powers I have ever seen in any magically inclined mortal. And that is saying a great deal. But she is the best this wretched little town had to offer me.”

“Well, then, maybe we’d better get along,” I said quickly. “Before her powers evaporate, or whatever. Listen, Vincent, this is what I wanted to say to you.

“You’ve got to save Brooke. Isn’t there some way you can take away her vampireness?”

At the word *vampireness*, Voldar flinched. Then I saw him nod slowly, as though things were suddenly beginning to make sense to him.

"There could be," Vincent answered levelly, "but I am not aware that I have 'got' to do anything for you, Meg."

"I—I didn't mean to sound bossy," I apologized. "I guess what I meant to say was please, please, can't you help her?"

"Why should I?" asked Vincent.

"Because she's my best friend." My voice was cracking with emotion.

"And *you*, Meg, are my worst enemy," Vincent replied.

I took a deep breath. "I know I am. I know it. But that shouldn't keep us from making a deal."

"A deal?" he asked tauntingly. "What could *you* possibly have to offer me, you puny child?"

"I don't know," I admitted. "But I'm willing to do anything if it will save Brooke."

"Even if it means becoming a vampire yourself?" asked Vincent.

Brooke's eyes widened. "Don't say yes, Meg!" she begged. "It's not worth it. You can't—"

But I was staring Vincent straight in the eye. "Even if it means becoming a vampire myself," I said firmly.

There was a long pause. I could hear the clock in the hall ticking steadily, and Pooch kicking some kitty litter around. Dumb cat! Didn't he realize this was too serious a time to visit the litter box?

"You know nothing, Meg," Vincent told me levelly. "Nothing of what it means to be a vampire. Let me show you, and then we shall see what you think."

Before I could reply, something that felt like a bolt of electricity zizzed through my body—and my blood froze. This time I *do* mean that literally. I could *feel* my blood freezing.

Everything inside me seemed to stop working.

I could feel my heart slowing from a normal beat to a dull, monotonous thud. I stopped breathing, stopped needing to breathe. When I blinked, dragging my eyelids open again was the hardest work I had ever done.

It was like being half-dead. And it wasn't a painful sensation, just strange. Somewhere deep in my brain a tiny leftover fragment of my real self thought, "Hey, this is weird!" But the rest of me just waited dully for whatever was going to happen next.

What came next was a fierce, throbbing thirst. At first it was just an itch at the back of my throat, something I could easily have ignored. Within seconds, though, it was all I could think about. My mouth felt as dry and parched as a dead leaf. *Drink, drink, drink,* my brain clamored. Gallons and gallons of liquid could have poured down my throat, and it would never have been enough.

I say "liquid" because it was blood I needed, not water. Somehow I knew that even though I had never tasted blood before. But where could I find blood? I knew two of the beings in the room with me couldn't supply it. They were vampires themselves. And the third was stronger than I; he'd be able to fight me off too easily.

My brother was sleeping upstairs, though. . . .

No. Of course I wouldn't touch Trevor. I could resist *that,* at least.

No, I couldn't. The great tide of thirst was stronger than any moral qualms I might have had. Nothing mattered except quenching it.

As if in a dream, I turned and walked out of my room. I could hardly walk, I felt so sick and weak. I put my hand on Trevor's doorknob, turned it, and walked floatingly toward his bed.

My brother looked very young lying there. I could smell the blood in his veins. I knew how hideously wrong this was, but I couldn't stop myself. Nothing had ever smelled so delicious. I tiptoed up to Trevor, bared my teeth, and prepared to—

"*No!*" I gasped, wrenching myself back from Trevor's bed. And at the sound of my voice the vision disappeared.

I was back in the living room, staring dazedly at Minerva and Brooke. I felt dizzy, but the terrible thirst was gone.

"It—it didn't happen," I said wonderingly. "Oh, thank heaven. I really thought I was going to—"

"Now you see what it is like," Vincent cut in sternly. "Can you honestly say you would make this sacrifice to save your friend?"

I couldn't answer for a second. Could I say that?

But did I really have a choice? If Brooke stayed a vampire, she was sure to bite me sooner or later. Besides, Vincent hadn't said I *had* to become a vampire in order to save Brooke. He had just asked if I was *willing* to become one. So it wasn't positively sure that saying yes would turn me into a vampire. ...

"I'll risk it," I said aloud. The words came out almost before I had meant them to—but once they were out, I was glad.

"Perhaps I will help you after all," Vincent said at last.

"You ... will?" I squeaked.

"Perhaps. It might be amusing in ways neither of us can predict. Yes," Vincent mused, "the idea definitely has its amusing side."

I didn't like the sound of that, but I kept my mouth shut. Even if he'd been willing to tell me what was so amusing, I didn't want to hear.

"The idea offers quite a few possibilities, in fact," Vincent went on. "I believe there is an English saying that expresses it well."

"What saying?" I asked nervously.

"The saying goes, 'There is more than one way to skin a cat.' " Vincent drew a deep breath and let it out very slowly. "Yes. I will help."

Brooke slid to the floor and lay facedown.

"Brooke!" I gasped. "Voldar, is she . . . she's still alive, isn't she?"

He was already kneeling next to her and gently turning her over. "She has only fainted," he said with relief. "But I think I must get her home, Meg. Surely this atmosphere cannot be healthy for her. Whatever has happened to Brooke has taken a terrible toll."

I turned to Vincent-Minerva. "Does Brooke have to be here for you to help her?"

"Yes," he replied tersely. "So let us continue. There is a favor you can do for me, Meg. You risk your life in doing it, of course."

"Of course," I said stoutly. "I didn't think you wanted me to make you a sandwich or something." I squared my shoulders, hoping I looked brave. "What's the favor?"

"I cannot tell you in this form."

My mouth dropped open. "You can't?" I said. "Why?"

"I do not have the strength to make the flimsy body of this medium bend to my will. I will need to leave her body first. Also," he added in a more practical voice, "I need to draw you a map."

"A map?" I echoed idiotically.

"A map," Vincent repeated. "And now I must take my leave. Written instructions will appear on your desk. Watch for them."

"I sure will," I said. "And thanks so much, Vincent. I promise I'll do whatever you say."

He laughed hollowly. "Of course you will. If you do not, your friend will become a vampire again. And I can guarantee that the first person she attacks will be you."

I still think it was unfair of him to tell me that. I had every intention of doing what he asked anyway. He didn't have to make it this big threat!

"And now—" Vincent's voice was turning thinner. "Now I take my leave. Goodbye, Meg. You are not quite as stupid as you appear."

"Gee, thanks," I whispered. Then suddenly I remembered something. "Oh, Vincent! Just one more thing!"

"Yes?" The voice seemed to come from far away.

"Can you move out of our house now?"

I thought I heard him chuckle. "I will pack my bags immediately."

Then he said no more.

But a diabolical cackling filled the air. It was so loud it made the house vibrate. Voldar and I clutched our ears and doubled up in pain. Then the sound gradually faded—and became a silly giggle.

A *giggle?*

Suddenly I realized that Minerva was the one who was giggling. "Oh, my," she said foolishly, in her normal voice. "What is going on here?"

As Voldar and I watched—I had to wonder what he was thinking of all this!—Minerva's face slowly bubbled back to normal. She shuddered. Her head spun around a few times. And then she uttered a loud, normal sneeze.

"Did it work?" she said brightly.

"Yes," Voldar and I said in unison.

"Good! Great!" Minerva sounded both thrilled and surprised. "Well, let me just write out a bill, and then I'll be toddling home. I'll get my pocketbook—it's out in the hall."

She had hardly left the room when Brooke began to stir. "Meg?" she murmured.

"I'm here," I said quickly, kneeling down beside her. "How are you?"

It was like watching a black-and-white TV picture slowly turn to color. Brooke's gray face began to turn pink. Her hollow cheeks filled out again, like bread-dough rising in a bowl. She opened her eyes, and I saw with relief that they were Brooke's nice green eyes once more, not the horrible red orbs I had seen the night before.

"You're okay again!" I gasped.

"Of course I am," Brooke replied sturdily. She pushed herself up on her elbows. "What am I doing on the floor?" she asked in amazement. "And what's Voldar doing here? I thought we were supposed to be having a sleepover!"

"We are," I said with a slightly crazed laugh. "We are. There was just a little . . . interruption. That's all."

After I'd paid Minerva (well, at least I had enough money left for *one* ski), we made Voldar stay for a cup of hot chocolate. Then he said courteously that it was time for him to be going home. "Since Brooke is herself again, I should leave you to your fun."

"I'll walk you to the door," I offered quickly.

At the front door I said, "There's some stuff I need to explain to you."

"There certainly is," said Voldar with a smile. "I believe I have understood some of it. Nevertheless, we definitely must talk soon."

"I'll call you tomorrow," I promised. "I'm sure Brooke will want to talk to you about a few things, too. But first I'll fill her in on what happened tonight."

Brooke and I had stayed up late on other sleepovers. But I had a feeling that this time we'd be doing just what Mom had warned me not to do before she left.

"Now, don't talk all night!" she had told me.

Chapter Thirteen

Of course all I could think about the next day was Vincent's message. Everything that happened to me seemed like a signal.

Was that tapping on my desk a message in vampirish Morse code? Oh, no, it was just the kid in front of me tapping on *his* desk.

Was the strange expression on a lunch lady's face the sign that she was about to channel Vincent? No, it turned out that she had just found a shoelace in the minestrone.

It went on like that all day. That evening, while I was halfheartedly catching up on some homework, the message finally came.

I was trying to figure out the area of a circle when my hand suddenly jerked, trembled, and began writing something entirely different. This time I wasn't nearly as frightened as I had been before. I guessed that Vincent was giving me his message—and that's what happened.

Again I read the words written in Vincent's thin, spiky cursive.

Travel to Drazylvonia. "Great," I muttered. "That should be easy."

I shall take care of the details. Leave them to me.

Vincent didn't seem like a very reliable travel agent. . . .

Pick a sprig of death's-head thyme.

I hoped I'd be able to find someone who could tell me what it looked like.

In the hour before sunset—be certain of the time—bring the thyme to the dungeon in Castle Vladestan.

What was Castle Vladestan?

In the dungeon you will find seven coffins belonging to the seven vampire leaders of Drazylvonia.

Oh, no.

Open the largest coffin.

No.

Inside the coffin you will find a vampire. Place the death's-head thyme in his hand. This will give him the desired message from me.

Close the coffin and leave quickly, before the sun sets.

That part, at least, I had no trouble with. But everything else . . .

I shall now draw you a map of the castle's location in Drazylvonia.

Quickly my hand, directed by Vincent, sketched a rough map at the bottom of the page. As far as I could tell, Castle Vladestan was smack in the middle of the Carpathian Mountains. Which would mean that even if I could find a way to Drazylvonia, I would still have a nearimpossible time finding the castle. (I was pretty sure that Drazylvonia didn't have many of those monorails you see in theme parks to help me out.)

I couldn't give in. I *had* to do this favor for Vincent. But at that moment I could see no way now. I'd have to wait and see exactly what Vincent meant by "taking care of the details."

On top of that, I was going to have to copy my homework over again. I'd never be able to explain to my teacher why I had drawn a map of Drazylvonia all over my geometry.

Brooke, Voldar, and I had a long talk at Brooke's house after school the next day. Now that I knew Voldar wasn't a vampire, he seemed much nicer, though I doubt *anyone* would have thought he seemed more normal. For example, he was busily hooking a severed chicken's foot up to a nine-volt battery while he talked to me and Brooke. "I want to test the reflexes," he said matter-of-factly. "Perhaps someday I will discover the secret of re-animating lifeless forms."

"Where did you find that thing, anyway?" I asked.

"At the grocery store. They sell chicken feet for soup, you know."

"Great. Battery-powered soup," Brooke answered with a shudder.

"Extra credit," Voldar said with a little shrug.

Brooke had already filled Voldar in on some of the things that had been going on, so now it was my turn. I had a million questions for him, and I decided to get the most embarrassing one out of the way first.

"You remember when I was snooping around in your room?" I asked awkwardly, averting my eyes from the chicken foot's twitching toes.

"Indeed I do. You found a box of dirt, I recall," Voldar said.

"That's right. Voldar, why did you *have* that dirt?"

"Sentimental reasons, merely. It is a custom in my country: When traveling, you bring a handful of Drazylvonian soil to remind you of your homeland. That way, however far from home you may travel, there is always part of Drazylvonia with you."

That made sense. "Another question. Why did my name sound familiar to you? I figured it was because you had heard it from other vampires or something."

"Well, no. I assume that Brooke's mother must have mentioned you to me when she was driving me to school that first day. In my confusion at being so new, I forgot that I had heard the name from her."

"Okay. Now, what on earth were you doing when I found you climbing the side of the school?"

It was Voldar's turn to look embarrassed. He looked down and made the chicken's foot do a little tap dance. "I fear I was showing off, Meg. In my town in Drazylvonia, I am well known as a rock climber. I had promised to demonstrate this skill to one of my new classmates, and I was practicing when you saw me. What else would you like to know, Meg?"

"How you got so *huge* and scary when I caught you on the wall. I swear, you were twice as tall as usual!"

"Oh, that? That is the simplest of tricks," said Voldar. "One of my hobbies at home is contortionism. It is simply a matter of stretching the muscles." For just a second he popped his head way up into the air and then down again. He looked like a retractable jack-in-the-box. "I am far more limber than the average person," he told me, unnecessarily.

"As far as scaring you," he continued, "I regret it. I was merely startled at having been caught. And I feared that you would tell someone in charge about my trick. I did not wish to get into trouble such a short time after my visit."

"Oh, I wouldn't have told," I assured him, "and you wouldn't have gotten into trouble, anyway. Mrs. Schultz

would have been mad at *me* for not accepting that people have different customs where you come from."

You know, customs like electrifying chickens' claws.

"Which would hardly be fair of her," Voldar pointed out, "given the fact that every day she tries to persuade me to go out for a team sport. I do not feel comfortable with this idea."

I stifled a giggle and turned so that I wouldn't have to meet Brooke's eye. "I can't quite see it myself," I managed to say.

I couldn't think of a single other thing to ask Voldar—oh, by the way, he dressed in black because black is *in* in Drazylvonia. And he also explained that the ring he'd given Brooke was of a type very common back home. "Well, I guess that's it," I said. "Thanks for being so patient."

"The pleasure was all mine," said Voldar. To my great relief, he covered the chicken foot and the battery with a black cloth. "And now I must ask you—what was the bargain you struck with Vincent? What are his terms?"

"Oh, it's much too complicated to go into now," I said quickly. "And besides, I'm sick of talking about vampires. Aren't you guys?"

Both of them nodded.

"You know, Voldar," I said, to change the subject, "I bet Brooke hasn't shown you one of the most important American customs."

"She has been so helpful that I find that impossible to believe," said Voldar. He smiled tenderly at Brooke. "What were you planning to say?"

"Rigging people's lockers," I said promptly. "Tomorrow, let's rig Miriam Charney's. Maybe you could even put that chicken foot in it, Voldar."

Well, that certainly got us away from a topic I didn't want to discuss. It wasn't that I minded telling *Voldar* what Vincent had asked me. It was that I didn't want Brooke to know about it. If she found out how hard—how horrible—how *impossible* the task ahead of me was going to be, I was afraid she'd get depressed all over again. And I didn't want that to happen. It was too much fun having her back to normal.

At breakfast a few mornings later I noticed that my parents were eyeing me and Trevor strangely. I wondered uneasily whether they could tell that something had happened. They could never have guessed what the something was, but were we in trouble anyway?

"Is—is everything okay?" I asked.

"That depends on you," my father answered, and my heart sank. So we *were* in trouble.

"I got kind of an unusual offer," Dad went on. "I met the editor of a travel magazine, and she told me they were looking for someone to write a piece about winter in the Carpathian Mountains. Apparently it's quite wild and beautiful there in the winter.

"Well, I told the editor it sounded great but that I didn't know any travel writers. And for some reason"—Dad shook his head—"she said she thought *I* would be perfect for it. I explained that I was a screenwriter, not a journalist, and she said, 'Then you'd be even *more* perfect! You'd see everything with a fresh eye!' Whatever *that* means. And then she mentioned what they were planning to pay."

Dad cleared his throat and glanced over at my mother. "So the bottom line is, kids, I took the assignment. And I'm going to the Carpathian Mountains at Christmastime."

The Carpathian Mountains. Vincent's homeland. And Voldar's.

"There's a little country called Drazylvonia in the heart of the mountains, and that's where I'll be staying," Dad continued.

"*You're* going to Drazylvonia?" I gasped at the same time that my brother knocked over his orange juice and wailed, "We're not going to have Christmas *together?*"

"Yes, Meg, and no, Trevor," Mom spoke up. "Not unless . . . kids, I know this is asking a lot, but if you would agree to come to Drazylvonia, we could all be together for Christmas. I know it would be a lot different from our regular Christmases here, but I'm sure we could have fun. We could ski, and go hiking in the woods, and see all the old castles there, and—well, *I* think it would be a great opportunity for all of us. And, Meg, you'd even have a friend. Isn't that nice Drazylvonian boy going home for Christmas, too?"

I nodded.

"So you'd have someone your own age to do things with!" Mom said triumphantly.

"What's more, the magazine will pay for the three of you to come along," my father put in. "That's *very* unusual for a magazine to do. This whole thing seems almost like a fairy tale to me."

A fairy tale, and a horror story. Yes, things were working out perfectly. Somehow, Vincent had arranged it to make sure that I would be able to keep my half of the bargain. But what awaited me in that desolate part of the world?

"A bargain is a bargain." I must have said the words out loud without realizing it, because Dad asked, "What's that, Meg?"

"I mean," I said hastily, "you've made a bargain with this editor, and it seems crazy of us not to come along. Don't you think so, too, Trevor?"

"I—I guess so. As long as we still get presents."

"Of course you'll still get presents!" Mom told him. "We can bring them with us!"

Trevor looked innocently at her. "And since we'll be so far away from home, we'll have to get lots of extra presents. Right?"

"Oh, absolutely. Lots of them," Mom said with a laugh. "I'm sure there will be all *kinds* of surprises waiting for you."

I was sure of that, too.

"I will be in my own home at that time," Voldar said the next morning at school. He had come to talk to me at my locker. "Perhaps I may assist you in your mission."

I sighed as I tried to arrange my books into some kind of carryable pile. "I don't even want to *think* about my mission. Besides, haven't you been dragged into enough vampire stuff already? I should think you'd just want to go home and play video games, or whatever you do over there."

"We do have video games in Drazylvonia," Voldar said with a smile, "but I have little interest in them. Believe me, it will be my pleasure to help you.

"You know," he went on thoughtfully, "you never did tell me what your mission is. What exactly did Vincent ask of you?"

"Well, it starts out okay." I gave up struggling with my books and threw a few of them back into my locker. "Something about picking a sprig of a plant called death thyme—"

"Death's-head thyme," Voldar supplied. "A well-known herb in Drazylvonia, famous for its poisonous qualities. And what do you do with this thyme?"

"That's the part that's not quite as much fun," I told him. "I have to take it to a castle that has a bunch of vampires in the basement. In the last hour before sunset I have to open the biggest vampire coffin and put the thyme into the"—I shuddered—"the hand of the vampire leader. It's supposed to send some kind of message to him from Vincent. Something about the power having passed from—"

To my surprise, Voldar shot out his hand and grabbed my wrist hard. "What is the name of this castle?" he asked hoarsely. "Did Vincent tell you?"

"Y-yes, he did. And let go of my wrist, you're hurting me. Anyway, he said it was called Castle Vladestan. Have you heard of it?"

"Its land borders that of my own home," Voldar muttered. I was startled to see that he was trembling.

"Voldar, that's a very weird coincidence," I said after a second.

"It certainly is," he replied.

For a moment we stared at each other, perplexed. Then I said, "But what's so bad about this castle? I mean, I've dealt with vampires before. There will be *more* vampires this time, but—"

Voldar interrupted me for a third time.

"I fear you have been misled, Meg," he said in a somber voice. "There is no hope of safety for anyone who sets foot inside Castle Vladestan. For five hundred years the castle has stood under a deadly curse."

He drew a deep breath. "No mortal who sets foot inside Castle Vladestan returns alive."

"Oh," I said.

I thought about that for a second.

"Hmmm," I added brilliantly.

"Well, I'm positive Vincent would never ask me to do something that would kill me," I finally said, hoping I was right.

I was pretty sure of that, anyway.

At least, I hoped I was right.

At least, I hoped I could trust Vincent not to—

I mean, at least I hoped that Vincent wouldn't ask me to do something that would *definitely* kill me.

ANN HODGMAN is a former children's book editor and the author of over twenty-five children's books, including the popular *My Babysitter Is a Vampire, My Babysitter Has Fangs,* and *My Babysitter Bites Again.* In addition to humorous fiction for children, she has written teen mysteries and non-fiction for reluctant readers. She is also a writer for *The Big Picture,* a series of educational posters distributed in schools nationwide.

JOHN PIERARD has illustrated the bestselling *My Teacher is an Alien* series and the *My Babysitter Is a Vampire* series. His pictures can also be found in several books in the *Time Machine* series and in *Isaac Asimov's Science Fiction Magazine.* He lives in Manhattan.

www.ingramcontent.com/pod-product-compliance
Lightning Source LLC
LaVergne TN
LVHW020640100826
845148LV00012B/2265

* 9 7 8 1 5 9 6 8 7 7 9 6 2 *